Love is
a time of enchantment:
in it all days are fair and all fields
green. Youth is blest by it,
old age made benign:
the eyes of love see
roses blooming in December,
and sunshine through rain. Verily
is the time of true-love
a time of enchantment — and
Oh! how eager is woman
to be bewitched!

A TANGLED WEB

Poppy James and Jill Squires work hard to build up their antique business in the market town of Foxbridge. One morning Miles Hatherford walks into the shop, causing Poppy to flee. Surely, after the disastrous way in which their romance had ended two years previously, he is no more eager to see Poppy than she is to see him — but she hasn't allowed for his charm and persistence . . . When Miles and Poppy go to live in London, they rent their cottage in Foxbridge to Chris Langton, who, Jill decides, is a vain, self-centred male chauvinist. At last, there are changes in Jill's somewhat lonely life, with new people around her and the Church Fete to organise.

Books by Julia Ashwell
in the Ulverscroft Large Print Series:

A FAMILY AFFAIR
AN IRRESISTIBLE FORCE

JULIA ASHWELL

◆

A TANGLED WEB

Complete and Unabridged

ULVERSCROFT
Leicester

First published in Great Britain

First Large Print Edition
published August 1995

British Library CIP Data

Ashwell, Julia
A tangled web.—Large print ed.—
Ulverscroft large print series: romance
I. Title
823.914 [F]

ISBN 0–7089–3343–2

Published by
F. A. Thorpe (Publishing) Ltd.
Anstey, Leicestershire
Set by Words & Graphics Ltd.
Anstey, Leicestershire
Printed and bound in Great Britain by
T. J. Press (Padstow) Ltd., Padstow, Cornwall

This book is printed on acid-free paper

Part One

Part One

1

POPPY JAMES was superstitious; not fanatically so but enough to believe that misfortunes came in threes. A puncture, and an enormous muddy stain on her raincoat sustained while changing the tyre, counted as two pieces of bad luck, and she waited apprehensively for the third.

"That cracked Dresden plate is worthless — smash that," her friend and colleague Jill advised.

"It doesn't count if you do it on purpose," Poppy argued.

A year ago Poppy had returned to her home town of Foxbridge to find Jill Squires on the point of selling the antique shop, which had become hers when her parents were killed in a boating accident. The debts she had also inherited were piling up and Jill, grief-stricken and unable to cope, had been at the end of her tether. Poppy, whose PR job in the Middle East had provided her with

3

a sensational salary but little opportunity to spend it, had immediately offered to buy a half share in the business.

Poppy and Jill were both twenty-four, had been born and raised in Foxbridge, and were strikingly attractive, but there the resemblance ended. Jill, blonde and sensible, was the stabilising influence on the partnership. Poppy, gypsy dark and impulsive, contributed flair and elan. It was she who dashed about the countryside, attending sales and buying stock, while Jill remained in the shop, doing the books and selling the results of Poppy's expeditions.

Poppy's initial knowledge of the antiques trade would have fitted easily on the back of a postage stamp but she was a fast learner. The combination of reference books, intuition and a helpless smile, which encouraged other dealers to pour out their expertise into her receptive ears, soon had her snapping up bargains and carrying them back to a delighted Jill.

On that particular morning Poppy should have been attending a sale twenty miles away but the puncture had delayed her and she decided not to bother. Thus it was that her first piece of bad luck was directly responsible for the third. Instead of bidding for bargains at Heathcote Manor, Poppy was in the shop when Miles Hatherford walked in.

The porcelain Buddha she had been dusting slipped from her nerveless fingers and the crash brought Jill hurrying from the office.

"Oh dear," she scolded, "couldn't you have indulged your superstitions on something less valuable? Do you want to clear up this mess while I attend to this gentleman?"

Poppy fled to the back of the shop and into the large, cobwebby cupboard which housed their utilities. She half closed the door and, with her ear to the gap, listened to the familiar murmur of Miles' voice, and Jill's laughing responses. Normally Jill was brisk and businesslike with customers but, then, few of them had Miles Hatherford's charm.

Two years ago he had charmed his way into Poppy's life and her heart.

The shop bell tinkled; the transaction was over and Jill came looking for her partner.

"Why are you hiding in the broom cupboard?"

"All sensible women should hide when Miles Hatherford comes into view," declared Poppy, emerging from her refuge.

"You know him?" Jill guessed.

"Of course I know him," Poppy snapped with uncharacteristic edginess. "I'm not in the habit of rubbishing complete strangers."

"But you didn't even speak to him."

Poppy went into the shop and began sweeping up the broken Buddha. "I'd rather have my jaws wired up than ever speak to him again."

"He gave you a bad time?" Jill guessed sympathetically.

"Oh, no, he gave me a marvellous time," Poppy retorted. "It was the greatest time of my life. I floated round on fluffy pink clouds for three months until I discovered that he was giving the same marvellous time to half the women in London."

"Only half the women?" Jill gently teased, hoping to humour her friend out of her obvious distress. "That makes him

6

quite faithful by today's standards."

Poppy shot the broken porcelain into a wastebin, clattered the brush and pan into the cupboard and flung herself into a chair, her lovely face distraught. Miles! What was he doing in a small Chiltern market town on a damp April morning? She couldn't recall his ever mentioning any connection with Foxbridge, so he couldn't be staying here. 'Please, let it be a one-off passing-through visit; please, even now, let him be cruising along the M40, London-bound with whatever he bought,' she silently prayed.

"What did he buy?" she asked with reluctant curiosity.

"The Victorian dresser," Jill replied, waving her hand towards the massive piece of furniture, "and he paid a deposit on the rosewood dining-table and chairs."

"Joe won't want to go traipsing up to London with that lot," Poppy said, anticipating the objections of their local carrier, "and, if he does go, he'll charge the earth."

Jill ran distracted fingers through her short fair hair, and Poppy experienced

7

a sudden sinking feeling. Jill rarely got ruffled, either physically or emotionally. "I've a feeling you're going to tell me something I don't want to hear."

"Joe won't have to go to London; just half a mile up the road. Mr Hatherford has bought Keeper's Cottage. Just as a weekend home, I think," she added hastily as Poppy's mobile features registered incredulity. "He told me he's not actually going to live there. I expect he'll just use it for weekends."

Poppy buried her face in her hands. "I don't believe it," she groaned. "This can't be happening."

Jill regarded her friend with exasperation. Poppy's dramatics were entertaining but she did sometimes go over the top. "It can't be that much of a disaster, love. Aren't you over-reacting just a teeny bit?"

Then Poppy lifted her head and Jill realised there was nothing phoney about her pale cheeks and stricken amber eyes.

"Crikey, he really did give you a bad time, didn't he? The beast!" she muttered. "I've a good mind to tell him what he can do with his money."

8

Then she looked at the generous amount on his carelessly scribbled cheque and common sense prevailed. "He's just paid this quarter's ground rent. There's the whole of Keeper's Cottage to furnish. We'll just have to try and look on him as our personal benevolent fund."

"Benevolent!" Poppy snorted. "He's that all right. Somebody should put a notice in the Foxbridge Gazette warning the local female population he's on the prowl."

"I imagine they'll all hear him when he starts baying at the moon," Jill said drily. "May I ask what he did that was so awful?"

"He ruined my life," Poppy wailed unhelpfully. "Why do you think I gave up a promising career in advertising to bury myself in Abu Dhabi? To get away from him, of course. Why do you think I'm here instead of in London? To avoid ever seeing him again. Not that I regret coming back," she tactfully added as Jill looked reproachful.

"London's a huge place," Jill reasoned. "Surely you could have avoided him?"

"I thought I was avoiding him by

coming back here," Poppy pointed out.

"Perhaps you were fated to meet again."

"Then fate has a lot to answer for," Poppy grumbled. "Via Miles Hatherford and his phoney promise of marriage it's turned me into a reclusive man-hater."

"Don't exaggerate," Jill said. "We're both reclusive because there's not much to do around here, and you don't hate any of the men we know."

"Only because they're all too boring to get emotional about," Poppy retorted. She took a shaky breath. "Do you mind if I try and revive myself with an early lunch?"

"Stay away from The Crown then," Jill advised, "just for today. Mr Hatherford mentioned he's staying there."

Poppy fetched her outdoor clothes and Jill watched, highly diverted, as she made fruitless efforts to disguise her striking looks. She stuffed her long dark hair beneath a felt trilby, pulled the brim down over her eyes and turned up the collar of her trench coat.

As she walked along the sparsely populated street, Poppy took advantage of a weak shaft of sunlight to don a pair of dark glasses which had lurked in her cluttered bag since last summer. They were hardly the most foolproof of disguises, but they gave her an added sense of security as she made her way towards The Three Feathers. It stood on the opposite side of the town square to The Crown Hotel and, imaging a blue laser stare directed at her from its windows, Poppy ran the last few steps and practically fell through the pub door.

'Hell's bells,' she thought. 'At this rate I'll be a nervous wreck before summer's over.'

The food at The Three Feathers was inferior to that at The Crown and, as Poppy moodily prodded at a plate of shepherd's pie, she added it to Miles Hatherford's growing list of misdemeanours.

'Of all the antique shops in all the towns all over the world, he walks into mine,' she thought. Surely, after the disastrous way in which their romance had ended, he was no more eager to see Poppy than she was to see him? He must have forgotten that this was her home town; he had probably forgotten her. No, no man could entirely forget a woman who had almost ruined his career.

"Hello, Poppy, long time no see." She sent her drink flying as a man slid into the vacant seat opposite her. "Sorry! Did I startle you? Let me get you another one. Chardonnet, right?"

"Thanks, Gordon." So much for her disguise! She managed to smile up into the anxious eyes of the youngest partner in a local firm of estate agents. He was one of the crowd of casual acquaintances with whom she and Jill socialised — if the occasional game of tennis or badminton and a drink afterwards could be called socialising.

While Gordon was at the bar, Poppy pulled off her hat and glasses and shook out her hair.

"There you are." Gordon appeared with a fresh drink for Poppy and a glass of lager for himself. "You don't usually eat here. Gone off The Crown?"

"Sort of," she evaded. "It doesn't do to get in a rut."

"It's hard not to in a place like

12

Foxbridge. I could never figure out why you came back once you'd escaped to London."

The answer was in The Crown Hotel or, possibly, poking around his new acquisition. Of course; Gordon might have handled the transaction and be in a position to enlighten her about Miles' plans.

"I hear that Keeper's Cottage has been sold at last," she said conversationally. "Some guy came into the shop this morning, buying furniture for it."

Gordon's pleasant but unremarkable face lit up. "Yes, the deal went through this week and they're starting to move in already. Nice chap, a Mr Hatherford. That's his car parked in front of The Crown."

Poppy glanced across the square to where a silver Jaguar was parked. It was the model Miles had promised himself if he received the promotion he was expecting, and Poppy felt a surge of relief that she hadn't inadvertently wrecked his career.

Gordon was still talking and something he said suddenly caught Poppy's attention.

"Did you say Mrs Hatherford?"

Gordon nodded. "He'll be spending the weekdays in town and just popping down here when he has time, but Mrs Hatherford will be living in the cottage full-time."

While Gordon rambled on, Poppy tried to assimilate the fact that Miles was married. To whom and for how long? Whoever it was, Poppy felt sorry for her — unless it was Sylvia Delgarth, of course. Those two deserved each other. But two years was a long time; time in which Miles could have met and married any number of women. Perhaps there was a child.

Poppy suddenly felt sick. Gordon was still talking and she wrenched her attention back to him. He had his head cocked on one side as though he had just asked her a question. Working on the theory that she had a fifty-fifty chance of giving the right answer, Poppy said brightly, "Yes, of course, Gordon."

He looked taken aback. "You will?"

"Er — will what?" she asked suspiciously.

"Have dinner with me on Saturday

evening," he repeated.

Jill was reduced to unladylike snorts of laughter when Poppy repeated this exchange to her. "You're going out with Gordon Field, the walking cliche? I don't believe it."

"Neither do I," Poppy muttered. "That'll teach me to pay more attention to what's going on. He was droning on and I was miles away, just nodding and shaking my head. I must have nodded when I should have shook."

Jill tried to look serious. "It could be worse. You've got to exorcise your prejudices some time — you might as well start with good old harmless Gordon. I presume Miles Hatherford is the reason you cold-shoulder every man who tries to date you?"

"Can you blame me? An experience like the one I had with him would have driven most women into a convent. I suppose you're right about Gordon. He's pretty harmless. I'd better buy something decent to wear. What would be appropriate to The Gourmet's Kitchen?"

Jill whistled. "Whew! Gordon is out to impress you. They allocate the tables according to how many designer labels you're wearing!"

Poppy looked down at her faded jeans and old jumper. "On my current form I won't rate a tray in the lobby. Perhaps I'll feel more enthusiastic about the whole grisly business if I buy something special."

When her partner had gone to lunch, Poppy stood in front of the mirror and tried to view herself objectively. Perhaps she was overdoing the casual image somewhat. When she had lived and worked in London, her wardrobe had been crammed with all the outfits necessary for her burgeoning career and busy social life.

It was during her time in the Middle East that Poppy discovered the bliss of being herself, without all the artificial props which had been such an essential part of her previous life-style. She grew her dark hair out of its fashionable crop and carefully cultivated a rich tan which made make-up superfluous.

She was still scowling at her reflection when Jill bustled back from lunch. "I've seen exactly the dress for you," she

16

enthused. "It's apricot crepe de chine, plain but beautifully cut."

"Where is this wondrous garment?"

"Ragamuffins'. It's an original, worth every penny," Jill rushed on as Poppy mimicked a fainting fit. "It's an investment."

"How can it be an investment if I'm only going to wear it once?" Poppy argued. She knew exactly what was going on in her friend's mind. She thought that once Poppy had broken the social ice, she would remain in the water. Fat chance!

But as she felt the luxurious dress settle over her slim curves like a silky second skin, she had to admit that Jill had terrific taste. The rich apricot was a perfect foil for Poppy's dramatic colouring, and the bias-cut flared skirt showed off her long legs to perfection. She emerged barefoot and self-conscious from the fitting room, and the assistant pounced on her with the usual gush of compliments.

For once they were justified and, as she twirled and caught sight of herself in the scattering of mirrors, Poppy felt a twinge of excitement. The fabric felt richly sensuous after months of slopping

17

around in casuals. And it was nice occasionally to dress up.

"It suits you beautifully, my dear."

Poppy smiled at her fellow customer. "You don't, by any chance, own shares in the shop?"

The woman laughed. "I wish I did. I'm clothes mad but I have to be circumspect at my age. When I was your age, clothing was rationed and money short. Now that I'm able to indulge myself, I have to stick to this sort of thing." She indicated the black velvet suit she was trying on.

"It's lovely," Poppy said truthfully. "It will look super with a high-necked white blouse and a spectacular brooch at the throat — a cameo, perhaps."

When they had completed their purchases, they fell into step and strolled along, chatting companionably. Poppy had the oddest feeling that they'd met before, but couldn't recall where or when. The woman certainly wasn't local, and Poppy found herself sneaking sideways glances at the upright, white-haired figure walking beside her, struck by the familiarity of the elegant profile

18

and bright blue eyes.

They eventually reached Squires Antiques and Poppy paused with her hand on the brightly polished brass door handle. "Well, this is where I leave you. Thank you for making up my mind about the dress."

"How lovely, to work in a place like this," her companion exclaimed. "I suppose you don't have any antique jewellery — a cameo, perhaps?"

Poppy's face flamed. "Oh, please, I wasn't trying to make a sale."

The woman patted her hand reassuringly. "I know you weren't, my dear, but I might as well give my business to you rather than some overpriced jeweller."

The bell brought Jill from the back office. She spotted the Ragamuffins' bag. "You bought it! Well done. That should have the waiters hovering around you at The Gourmet's Kitchen on Saturday night. I'm sorry — " she transferred her attention to Poppy's companion — "I didn't see you come in. May I help you?"

Poppy dumped the carrier bag on the counter. "It's all right, Jill. I'll attend

19

to this. Do we still have that Italian cameo?"

Jill unlocked the glass case which held their small collection of jewellery and brought the tray of brooches over to the counter. The cameo, pink and white in a silver filigree setting, glowed against the brown velvet pad, and the woman picked it up with an exclamation of pleasure.

"It's charming, and you're so right about it going with my new suit. Oh, I am doing well with my shopping! I was rather dubious about moving out of London. It's this dicky heart of mine; my ridiculous family think I should slow down and banished me to the country, but I really think I'm going to like it here."

Her enthusiasm was infectious and the two girls smiled at each other over her bent head.

"You must come and visit me — tea, or dinner, perhaps — when I've settled in," she went on, writing out a cheque for the brooch, "but I'm in chaos at the moment. Not a stick of my furniture looks right in my new lovely new home, so I'm having to start all over again, like a bride." She waved the cheque in the air to dry the ink. "You'll probably be having more of these from me. You have some beautiful old pieces. I love that dresser."

"It's sold," Poppy said regretfully; she would much rather it went to her new acquaintance than Miles Hatherford. "But I expect I could find you something similar."

"You are a clever girl," the woman said with her twinkling smile. "Now, perhaps you can point me towards a garden centre. My new garden is appallingly neglected. I thought I'd scatter a few packets of seeds about until I can get round to some serious weeding and pruning."

Poppy and Jill watched her slight, upright figure hurry past the window.

"What a sweet, dotty lady," Poppy said. "Her family must be mad if they think they can slow her down. I wonder who she is."

Jill glanced at the cheque and bit her lip. "Oh dear. Unless there's been a sudden, coincidental influx of people called Hatherford into town, I'm afraid that was your ex-future mother-in-law, Beatrice Hatherford."

So the new occupant of Keeper's Cottage was Miles mother, not his wife! In a way Poppy was relieved because it meant that Miles was less likely to spend every spare moment in Foxbridge. On the other hand, it placed her in an awkward position regarding her friendship with Mrs Hatherford. Imagine accepting an invitation to dine with her and sitting there in mortal dread that her son might walk in!

Beatrice Hatherford came into the shop twice more during the week, staying to share a cup of coffee with the girls, leaving behind cheques for items she had purchased and pressing invitations to visit her.

She frequently mentioned Miles, who was obviously the light of her life, and Poppy listened with reluctant fascination. He was still single and still living in the same block of service flats in Highgate. And, far from losing his job, he now had a seat on the board of Macuird International.

"I do wish he'd settle down," Miles'

mother sighed as she, Jill and Poppy stood admiring a chaise-longue she had just decided to buy. "I would so love some grandchildren, but I can't imagine any of those plastic-looking females he dates allowing inconvenient things like babies to upset their lives."

Her tone was scathing, and Poppy inwardly squirmed. Had she been like that? Would Beatrice Hatherford have dismissed Poppy as being plastic had they met two years ago? Perhaps she had been, although she didn't think so.

2

POPPY had met Miles, appropriately enough, on February the fourteenth. Her morning post had yielded four Valentines. One came from mother — who always sent one in case there were no others — and three from an assortment of would-be Lotharios at the advertising agency where she worked.

It was when she was leaving Holborn Station that it happened, just like in a TV commercial. The proverbial tall, dark and handsome stranger appeared in front of her, thrust a bunch of red roses into her hands and vanished into the crowd. There was a business card taped to the wrapping, with a scribbled message on the back, asking Poppy to telephone if she was free for dinner one night, any night.

Thinking about it months later, when disillusionment had set in, Poppy bitterly reflected that Miles had probably spent the early part of the morning repeating the mystery man act, and the rest of the day taking calls from the bedazzled recipients of his flowers. His florist bill must have been astronomical!

Poppy dithered, bewitched by the gesture and the man who had made it. It was the kind of thing that only happened once; a tiny precious moment to be stored in the memory and treasured like a faded pressed flower in an old album. No man could live up to the expectations promoted by such a gesture.

She spent the evening brooding over the various romantic disappointments she had experienced since coming to live in London, and decided to let the whole thing remain a pleasant memory which would provide her with an occasional fantasy about the mysterious stranger. Then, as she lay in bed that night, she kept picturing black-lashed blue eyes and a wide, smiling mouth.

The following morning she sat in her small cluttered office, staring at the roses and fingering the embossed card. Miles Hatherford — a nice name. And he was a departmental head at one of the largest export firms in the country, so he was neither a crook nor a fool. Poppy's hand hovered over the phone. Oh, what the heck! If she didn't like the sound of him, she would simply thank him for the flowers and hang up.

"Mr Hatherford? This is Miss James." Her low voice had somehow risen by an octave and, covering the receiver, she nervously cleared her throat.

"Miss James? Poppy James?" There was nothing wrong with his warm voice. "I'd just about given you up."

"But you don't know who I am," Poppy said, startled.

"You're Poppy James," he explained. "You're about five feet seven, slim, with short dark hair and legs that keep all the men in your railway carriage entertained every morning. As I'm not in the habit of picking up women in public places, I thought up yesterday's ploy to get to know you."

"I've never seen you on the train," she objected, unnerved to discover that a stranger had been observing her so closely.

He laughed. "I only use it if the traffic

looks impossible, and I don't connect until Oxford Circus. And I don't honestly think you'd notice if the train burst into flames. You're either reading or staring blankly at the advertisements."

Poppy joined in his chuckles. "I've discovered that it's best to avoid eye contact on public transport. But how do you know my name?"

"I read the luggage label on that small suitcase you sometimes carry on Fridays." Then, "Are you ringing to accept my invitation to dinner — please?"

It was this 'please' which decided Poppy. He sounded like a small boy about to be deprived of his favourite teddy bear. She was charmed into acquiescence. They arranged to meet the same evening and she mystified her colleagues by walking around all day sporting a silly grin. She knew, she just knew that this man was going to be different from all the other men she had dated. If she'd known how different she would have locked herself in the Ladies and refused to come out!

In the restaurant that evening she surreptitiously studied him, trying to analyse his appeal. He was tall and slim, with a lightly-muscled frame which indicated that, like many desk-bound men, he jogged or played squash to keep fit. His hair, which was as dark as her own, had the careful unruliness that only expensive styling can achieve, and his intelligent, slightly saturnine face was attractive without being remarkable except for vivid blue eyes accentuated by long dark lashes. There were more obviously handsome men in the restaurant, but Poppy noticed that their female companions kept casting appraising glances towards Miles.

As with most first dates, the conversation was exploratory; a cautious sounding out of each others tastes and opinions. Like herself, Miles was an only child, single and living along. He was thirty and cheerfully admitted to being ambitious.

"That's the big problem I have in my relationships with women," he explained. "I work long hours and frequently have to go away on business trips."

Poppy nodded coolly, noting the plurals in the first sentence. "I understand. I'm something of a workaholic myself."

"Oh dear — " he took her hand and

examined her long fingers and flawlessly manicured nails — "I do hope we manage to spend some time together."

Poppy hoped so, too. He was quite the most exciting thing that had happened to her since moving to London. She kept waiting for the catch — there was always a catch! — but he was charming, attentive and impeccably behaved.

One month and a dozen dates later she was convinced she was in love and, to her intense joy, Miles seemed to be equally besotted with her. They didn't meet nearly as often as she would have liked, but they were both working for promotion, and when they did meet it was well worth the wait.

The only cloud in Poppy's brilliant sky and, looking back, the one dark thread running through her relationship with Miles was the ambiguous relationship he had with his secretary.

Poppy's first encounter with her was on her fifth date with Miles. They had arranged to lunch together and play truant from work in the afternoon. Poppy was ready early and decided to surprise Miles at his office.

Macuird International occupied several floors in a brand-new tower block and Poppy was most impressed when she was directed to Mr Hatherford's suite. She opened the door which bore his name and found herself in a shiny chrome office which was occupied by an equally shiny chrome blonde. She raised a delicate eyebrow, obviously not rating Poppy the courtesy of a verbal greeting. Deciding that two could play at that game, Poppy gave her a brief, silent nod and headed for what she assumed was Miles' inner office.

"You can't go in there without an appointment." The blonde's voice matched her appearance: cold, brittle and efficient.

"But I have an appointment," Poppy said sweetly.

"Oh?" She sounded sceptical rather than surprised. She leafed through a diary the size of a Victorian family Bible. "And you are . . . ?"

"Poppy James."

"Oh yes, I see." Her laughter didn't warm her green eyes. "Miles gave me your details last week to put on my list; you know, where and when to send flowers and suchlike." She slid a folder out of her desk drawer. "Here we are: Poppy James." She read out Poppy's Holland Park address in tones which managed to imply that it was only a step up from a hostel for down and outs.

"List?" Poppy asked uneasily.

"Yes. His mother, the boss's wife, important lady clients and — er — others." She flashed her chilly smile again. "I do it for all my bosses. It gives them a little less to worry about."

"How thoughtful," Poppy said coldly, guessing that Miles' secretary was less interested in saving him worry than keeping tabs on his private life. "Perhaps you'll tell Mr Hatherford I'm here, Ms — er?"

"Sylvia Delgarth," she drawled, lifting the telephone. "Miles, a Miss James has arrived."

'She makes me sound like a parcel,' Poppy fumed, then Miles hurried out and she forgot her annoyance as he greeted her with a swift kiss.

"Hello, gorgeous. This is a lovely surprise. Have you decided where you want to go this afternoon?"

31

They turned to leave, then he dashed back into his office and returned carrying a small posy of violets. Poppy lifted the delicately scented flowers to her nose, looked at Ms Delgarth as if to say, "There, he doesn't need you to remind him to buy flowers for me," and was shaken by the venom in the other woman's eyes.

"She's a bit of a dragon, your secretary," she said to Miles as they strolled along the crowded pavement towards the trattoria where they were going to lunch.

"Really?" He looked surprised. "Well, she's very efficient. I'd be lost without her."

Poppy never got entirely used to Sylvia Delgarth's acid tongued hostility, but she grew an extra skin and patiently ran the gamut of bitchy remarks. It would have been easy to retaliate, but that would have brought her down to Sylvia's level. She was tempted to appeal to Miles to swap secretaries but, infuriatingly, Sylvia was all sweetness and light in his company, and Poppy had the uneasy feeling that Miles would think she was making a fuss about nothing.

The events which led to Poppy's hasty departure to the Middle East all took place within twenty-four hours of one another. Poppy had cooked dinner for them at her flat and, when she went into the kitchen to make coffee, Miles wandered out after her.

"I've had a brilliant idea," he murmured, nuzzling the back of her neck and causing her to spill coffee beans all over the work top.

"Miles, you're a menace," she protested, laughing. "Go and sit over there and tell me about your idea."

He scooped up the beans and put them in the grinder. "Have you fixed your summer holiday yet? I wondered if . . . Sir William, our Chairman, has bought a villa in Nice and placed it at the disposal of his heads of department. I wondered if — well, that is . . . ?"

Poppy bit her lip as she visualised her crammed business diary and the mountain of work on her desk. "I don't know. I — er . . . "

Miles mistook her hesitation. "Look,

darling, would you feel better about it if we made it our honeymoon?"

His tone was so diffident that Poppy wondered if she had imagined his question; that she had somehow projected her wishes into false reality. He looked at her quizzically and repeated his suggestion, and still she couldn't answer. Why not, it was the moment she had dreamed about for weeks, wasn't it?

"Darling, say something, even if it's only no."

"What?" she breathed, recovering herself. All thoughts of work vanished. "Oh yes, Miles, I'd love to marry you."

The following evening Macuird International were holding a reception for an overseas trade delegation and, as Poppy was accompanying their youngest and brightest executive, she pulled out every stop. Her dress cost two week's salary and it showed in every perfect detail. Made of scarlet silk jersey, it lovingly hugged Poppy's slender curves and showed off to perfection the contrast between her dark hair and creamy skin.

As she stood in the powder-room, checking her flawless make-up, Poppy smiled as she recalled Miles' delight at her appearance. She did so want to be a credit to him. She had just indulged in a final twirl and was about to join Miles in the banqueting room when Sylvia Delgarth walked in.

She gave Poppy a distainful glance and sneered, "I see you've been rummaging around Covent Garden Market again."

Poppy threw aside previous restraint. She eyed Sylvia's gold lame creation, which must have cost even more than her own dress, and said sweetly, "I took a leaf out of your book and went to Oxfam."

Sylvia drew in a sharp breath. "How dare you?"

Nothing, not even Sylvia, could upset Poppy tonight. "You'd better get used to it. You'll be seeing a lot more of me in future."

Sylvia feathered on a touch more gold eye shadow. "Oh, why's that? Miles given you a job, has he?"

"No, he's asked me to marry him."

Sylvia's mirthless, cut-glass laugh echoed around the room until Poppy began to fear for the safety of the long mirrors.

"Oh dear, I'm sorry," she finally said without a trace of apology in her voice, "but I wish I had a pound for every one of you little girls who've been taken in by Miles. I suppose he's sweet-talked you into going to Sir William's place in France. Poor Miles. It's unfortunate for him that you're one of the old-fashioned types who have to have a wedding ring dangled in front of them to make them feel virtuous about what they're doing."

Poppy didn't know which of Sylvia's mistakes to correct first. "What a horrible thing to say!" she gasped, her happiness and confidence crumbling. "Miles isn't like that."

"How can you possibly know what Miles is like?" Sylvia said scornfully. "You've been seeing him for a few months. I've known him for two years. Just think of all those foreign trips he takes me on! Miles collects silly women like you the way other men collect beer mats. It's his hobby, a way of feeding his ego. I put up with it because it keeps him happy and he always comes back to me."

Poppy felt the blood drain from her face.

"And," Sylvia gloated relentlessly, "he doesn't just use women for pleasure. How do you think he's done so well at Macuird's? Sir William's easily influenced by his wife and, if you've met Ruth Macuird, you must admit that she's a very attractive woman."

Poppy didn't wait to hear any more. She snatched up her bag and escaped into the lobby. Her first instinct was to run as far away as possible; away from Miles and his half-hearted promise of marriage; away from Sylvia's spiteful allegations.

Then Poppy's common sense took over and she knew that she had to give Miles the benefit of the doubt. It wouldn't solve anything to confront him with Sylvia's accusations; if they were true he would deny them, and if they were untrue he would think Poppy disloyal for listening to such tales. She would have to decide for herself what was the truth.

Slowly and reluctantly, Poppy walked through the open doors into the banqueting room. The smart assembly were standing in an informal half-circle around Sir William. He had evidently just made a speech and was beckoning for somebody to come forward. Poppy tried to stop her lip curling as Miles emerged from the throng, a modest, boyish smile on his face.

'Modest and boyish, my hat!' she raged to herself. 'They should know what he's like and how he works for his promotion.' It seemed to her that Lady Macuird, a pretty, modestly-dressed woman in her late thirties, was applauding with more enthusiasm than was justified.

But Poppy managed to contain her feelings and listened politely to Miles' gracious and humorous little speech accepting Macuird's annual award to its most successful sales manager. He made a general reference to his future, and looked at Poppy with such eloquence in his blue eyes that she felt a little of the ice around her heart melt.

But, despite her good intentions, Poppy had a miserable evening. She and Miles had agreed beforehand that it would be bad policy to spend the evening in each other's company. Poppy had been looking forward to meeting his colleagues and playing — somewhat prematurely — the good company wife. Now, as she forced herself to circulate and listen to endless waffle about pre-tax profit and long-term portfolios, she regretted their decision. She would far rather be at Miles side, hearing what it was he was saying to cause Lady Macuird such amusement.

Excusing herself to her companion, Poppy made her way across to them.

After introducing the two women, Miles said, "I can't stop thinking how utterly gorgeous you look tonight, darling. Doesn't she, Ruth?"

"Mm, I'll say." The older woman's eyes took in every detail of Poppy's appearance. "Can you imagine Billy letting me wear something as slinky as that, Miles? He's such an old prude. And it's not just me he's strict with — he plays the heavy father with his staff as well. Woe betide any of you whose standards don't measure up to his own."

The three of them automatically glanced across to where Sir William, a handsome man in his early fifties, was holding court among his staff.

The news that he was something of a Puritan came as a relief to Poppy. It reinforced the small sane voice which kept telling her she was foolish to believe Sylvia's malicious gossip. Apart from all the other considerations, Miles was far too ambitious to endanger his career with promiscuous behaviour. And it made Sylvia's other claim, the one implicating Lady Macuird, too ludicrous to contemplate.

Then Ruth Macuird possessively took Miles' arm, saying, "Miles dear, there's that Swedish banker I promised to introduce you to. You will excuse us, won't you?" She flashed Poppy a dazzling smile. "I must confess Miles is my favourite among all my husband's bright young men, and I like to look after his interests."

After that, Poppy's evening went from bad to worse. As she returned to her self-imposed task of socialising with Miles' colleagues, she watched with despair as it seemed that Miles was approached, spoken to and flirted with by every attractive woman in the room. Normally this wouldn't have bothered her, but Sylvia's cruel words had sown seeds of doubt and insecurity.

"You're very quiet," Miles said as they drew up in front of her block of flats. "You've hardly said a word to me all evening."

"I'm surprised you noticed," Poppy said dully. "You were so busy chatting up all those wives and secretaries and lady executives."

"Oh, come on, darling!" Miles scoffed. "I could say the same about you and all the men who were there tonight, but we both know it wasn't like that. We were doing a job, and you played your part very well."

"Thank you," Poppy whispered. She turned away as he tried to embrace her. "I have a rotten headache, Miles. I'll see you tomorrow night."

After a miserable, restless night Poppy decided that the only way she could set her mind at rest was to confront Miles with Sylvia's accusations. She would know by those expressive eyes whether or not he was telling her the truth. She might not like the outcome of their confrontation, but anything would be better than this awful nagging doubt.

When Poppy walked into Sylvia's office

the following lunch-time, the only trace of its occupant was the usual heavy pall of musky perfume. Poppy had phoned to make sure that Miles was free to see her; presumably Sylvia, not wishing to face Poppy, had gone to lunch.

The door to Miles' office was open. Poppy silently crossed the thickly-carpeted floor and paused on the threshold. Miles was standing with his back to her. Poppy was about to greet him but her voice died in her throat as a pair of hands slid up around his neck, the scarlet-tipped fingers cupping his head.

Miles moved slightly and Poppy saw the person who had previously been obscured by his height; Sylvia Delgarth, her green eyes carefully calculating Poppy's horrified reaction.

The next thing Poppy knew was being out in the corridor, her shaking fingers fumbling a plastic cup out of the water dispenser. It was all true, every revolting word of Sylvia's gossip about Miles.

"Meeting Miles for lunch, are you?"

Poppy jumped as Sir William appeared at her side. "Er . . . "

"I won't keep him long, my dear, but

I must have a quick word," and with a flourish of the folder he was carrying, Sir William went into Miles' outer office.

Poppy could have stopped him, she decided when she thought about it afterwards. She could have chased after Sir William and staged a loud conversation with him, warning Miles and Sylvia that they were not alone, but she didn't. She just stood there, rooted to the spot, and let Miles' strait-laced boss walk through into the inner office.

3

POPPY glanced around in amusement at the pretentious decor of The Gourmet's Kitchen; a mixture of Provencal and Olde Englishe, with strings of onions and garlic, and distressed oak furniture. Fortunately the owner's choice of chef was more discriminating and Poppy could understand why the round, slightly wobbly tables had to be reserved well in advance.

"Poppy, you look absolutely super," Gordon said as they seated themselves at a table near the tiny dance floor, and she fought back the eerie sensation that she was about to have a midnight feast with an overgrown schoolboy.

The food was worth every penny of the hair-raising prices, Gordon's conversation was undemanding without being boring, and Poppy began to unwind and enjoy herself. Perhaps Jill was right: once Poppy began socialising again she might acquire a taste for it. While the waiter was serving coffee, she went to the powder-room.

"I told you that dress was perfect for you."

Poppy turned and found herself faced with Beatrice Hatherford. She smiled with genuine warmth. "How nice to see you! This is a coincidence."

"Not really," the older woman replied with a mischievous smile. "I recalled Jill mentioning that you were coming here so I did some crafty manoeuvring. I can't seem to persuade you to dine at the cottage, and I do so want you to meet my son. I suppose you think me a silly old woman, but I'm sure you and Miles will like each other."

As Miles' mother chattered on, extolling his virtues, Poppy stared at herself in the mirror and willed her face to maintain its pleasant, interested expression. It wasn't easy.

"Does your son know about your — er, manoeuvring? He might not approve."

Beatrice chuckled. "Miles spoils me. Ever since I developed this dicky heart, he indulges my every whim. Not that I have many. But occasionally I take a tiny

45

advantage of my condition, like tonight, for instance."

"Oh," Poppy said weakly, unable to think of a sensible reply.

Her companion misinterpreted Poppy's lack of joy at the prospect of meeting Miles. "Oh dear, you're probably with some young man. I must be making an absolute pest of myself, playing the pushy mother. You don't wear a ring, so I assumed you were unattached."

"I am," Poppy admitted without thinking. "Gordon is just a friend." A thought struck her. "Does your son know why he's here tonight?"

Beatrice stared innocently down at the toes of her black patent shoes. "You mean, does he know I'm conniving a meeting between the two of you? Yes, he does — sort of. He's heard me nattering on about my two young friends in the antique shop and he laughed when I mentioned that you might be here tonight. I'm afraid I'm not very subtle."

But Miles had seen Poppy that first time he came into the shop. He must think he was meeting Jill.

46

"Jill served him when he bought your dresser. He'll be disappointed if he's expecting her."

"Oh no. He asked if it was the pretty blonde and I said, 'No, the even prettier brunette.'"

The compliment was lost on Poppy as she examined her reflection again. Shoulder-length hair, tanned skin with no make-up; she was very different from the crop-haired fashion plate she had been in London. Miles obviously hadn't recognised her in the dimly-lit shop.

She became conscious that the other woman was looking at her curiously, and she managed a shaky laugh. "I'm sorry, Mrs Hatherford, I . . . " She took a deep breath and crossed her fingers firmly behind her back. "I'm afraid I told a tiny fib about Gordon. We are slightly more than friends but — " her fertile imagination took flight — "our families don't get on, so when we're in public together, we try not to look too — er — "

"Affectionate?" her companion suggested. "How romantic — like Romeo and Juliet."

"Quite," Poppy murmured, trying not to snigger as she envisaged Gordon's sturdy legs clad in colourful medieval hose. "So you see, I'm afraid I'm a lost cause as far as your son is concerned."

"What a shame! I am trying so hard to wean him away from those awful plastic females he dates. Still, you never know, do you?" Miles' mother said ambiguously. She evidently didn't think it possible that any man could be more desirable than her son. "We'd better be going. I've kept you chatting far too long."

Poppy accompanied her to the exit, hoping that her new image and the dim lighting would continue to preserve her anonymity. Once through the door, she flashed Beatrice a quick smile and, her gaze fixed firmly ahead, marched to where Gordon was patiently waiting.

"I ordered a couple of brandies, Poppy,"

"Lovely, Gordon."

With a fond smile which she hoped wouldn't frighten Gordon to death, or give him mistaken ideas, she raised her glass. "What shall we drink to? How

48

about health, wealth and happiness?"

"I say, that's a bit ambitious. Tell you what, the cricket season starts next week. Let's drink to the team. I'm captain this year, you know."

"To the Foxbridge cricket team," Poppy solemnly intoned, clinking her glass against Gordon's and hoping that the Hatherfords weren't within earshot. This was hardly the stuff of thwarted romance!

"Would you like to dance, Poppy?"

She had accepted before realising that she was making herself the perfect target for the sharp blue gaze which would pick her out like a sniper's rifle. On the dance floor, she snuggled up to Gordon and buried her face in his shoulder.

He tensed at the close contact. "I say, steady on, Poppy."

She unglued herself from his solid frame and shook her hair over her face instead. "Sorry, Gordon. Nothing personal."

She kept her eyes fixed firmly on his lapel, working on the ostrich theory that if she didn't see Miles, he wouldn't see her. She hoped that, whatever his feelings towards her, he wouldn't enlighten his mother about their ill-starred romance two years ago. Or, if he did, he would gloss over the less palatable details.

The music stopped. There was a smattering of applause and some jostling as the dancers moved to leave the cramped floor. Poppy bent to adjust her sandal strap, at the same time grabbing Gordon's sleeve to prevent him from leaving. She felt safer in the dark anonymity of the dance floor.

The band launched itself into a slow number. Poppy slid into her companion's arms and blinked with surprise. Surely Gordon's suit was a conservative Prince of Wales check, not pale grey worsted with hand-stitched lapels?

"Just keep dancing, Poppy," Miles' voice advised her as she tensed in protest, "unless you'd like an undignified public scene."

Numb with shock, Poppy obeyed, not daring to raise her eyes. If she did she would see Miles and know it was really him and not a cruel trick being played upon her by her senses.

She eventually found her voice. "You

50

wouldn't dare, not in front of your mother."

"True," he admitted, "but there are other times and places."

Poppy worked up the nerve to look at him and was deeply shaken by the sense of déjà vu which swept over her. His face was still as familiar to her as her own and she felt her dislike of him deepen, if that was possible. Because of him she had never been able to have a fulfilling relationship with any other man; had never wanted to. His lips were curved in an appropriately sociable smile but his eyes were like blue ice.

"What are you doing?" Poppy hissed.

"I would have thought . . ."

"Smile," he ordered her.

She followed his gaze and managed a pale smile for Beatrice, who was fondly watching their progress from a table at the edge of the floor.

"Does she know about us?" Poppy asked fearfully.

"No. I've never discussed you with her. She does have a weak heart."

"Are you blaming me for what happened?"

51

"Nothing happened, but that was no thanks to you." Several people glanced curiously at them and Miles lowered his voice. "You just stood there and let my strait-laced boss, of all people, walk in on what looked like a very compromising scene. Sylvia said you did it deliberately, and then walked away. If you'd bothered to wait I could have explained, as I did to Sir William, that I was comforting Sylvia because she'd lost her pet cat."

Poppy let out a snort that had heads turning their way again. "Sir William might have believed you but I doubt if I would. And it wasn't just that, it was . . . Oh, what's the point? I suppose we're going through this charade to please your mother?"

"Yes. She misguidedly thought we might take a liking to each other."

"Fat chance!"

The dance ended and they stepped apart, glowering at each other. Poppy turned to go and Miles grabbed her arm. "Hang on, I have something to ask you."

"Too bad. I've done my good deed for the day. If you have anything else

52

to say, send me a letter." Poppy shook off his restraining hand and returned to her table.

"Nice chap, isn't he?" said Gordon.

"Terrific," Poppy agreed through clenched teeth. "May we go, please, Gordon?"

'Home' was the flat over Squire's Antiques, which she shared with Jill. After thanking Gordon for a lovely evening — well, most of it had been — she let herself in the side door and ran upstairs to where Jill was already in bed.

She stopped sniffling over Tess of the D'Urbervilles and looked expectantly at Poppy. "Well?"

"Not very," Poppy said gloomily, flopping down on the end of the bed.

Jill waited, burning with curiosity but not wanting to pry. "Great food at The Gourmet's Kitchen, isn't it?"

"I suppose so," Poppy mumbled.

"What's the matter, love?" Jill said with concern. "Did Gordon get out of hand?"

"Think of something more unlikely," Poppy challenged her.

"I can't."

"The Hatherfords were both there: mother and son."

Jill groaned with sympathy. "Oh no, poor you. Don't tell me: dear old Beatrice is matchmaking, right? She's dropped enough hints when she's been in the shop."

"Right. She admits it, too. She cornered me in the powder room and, out of sheer self-defence, I ended up telling her some cock-and-bull story about me and Gordon being practically engaged but keeping it secret because our families wouldn't approve."

"You are an idiot," Jill scolded. "You're bound to be caught out in the end."

"Not if I can help it," Poppy said grimly, stalking off to bed.

She pulled off the expensive dress, tossed it carelessly over a chair and climbed into her striped cotton night shirt. She settled down beneath the duvet, then leapt out of bed again and grabbed her elderly teddy bear from his usual seat on the dressing-table. There were some nights when a girl couldn't be expected to sleep alone.

Disjointed scenes and snatches of conversation whirled around in her head as she wondered how she could cope with this latest crisis. Her life had collapsed once before. She had painfully rebuilt it and, just when she thought that she had achieved a kind of happiness, the architect of the first disaster had appeared again and was threatening another demolition job.

On the first occasion she had run, but not this time. Why should she? What, in the final analysis, did she have to fear from Miles? She could live with the way he felt about her; he wasn't the only person with whom she didn't get on. Only a saint was universally popular, and Poppy was just a normal human being.

But what about his mother? Poppy couldn't go around cold shouldering her. And what would she think if she discovered that Poppy hadn't been completely truthful about Gordon? It was a small community — nothing stayed secret for long.

Poppy got out of bed and went back to Jill's room. "I wish I hadn't told Mrs Hatherford that fib about Gordon. She's such a sweetie. What will she think of me if she finds out?"

"The same as the rest of us," Jill said, not too sympathetically, "that you're stark, raving mad. Why don't you put your brain into gear before opening your mouth?"

"Mind you," Poppy brooded, ignoring the insult, "I suppose Miles has every right to be just as mad with me, after what I did."

She rose to leave and Jill screeched, "Poppy! I know we don't pry into each other's business, but you can't say something like that and then walk off and leave me all agog — I shan't sleep."

Poppy hesitated, not wanting to open old wounds. Then she relented and, seating herself on Jill's bed again, gave her an account of her disastrous romance with Miles. It was the first time she had spoken about it to anyone and she found it a painful, humiliating experience. When she had finished, she sat back and waited for the soothing balm of her friend's sympathy, but Jill merely looked puzzled.

"Didn't you ever confront Miles with the dreadful things this Sylvia person said about him? About his being a womaniser, I mean?"

"And have to listen to more of his lies?" Poppy exploded. "No way! Besides, it all fits; the business trips with Sylvia; the way Lady Macuird behaved. And the day I walked in on him and Sylvia in his office . . . " Poppy's voice wobbled. "Pet cat, indeed! The only pet Sylvia would have had was a vulture."

"So he never knew why you walked out on him and flounced off to Abu Dhabi?"

"Sylvia saw me watching them; she'd have enjoyed telling him."

"But didn't he attempt to get in touch with you?" Jill persisted. "It sounds as though he was genuinely fond of you . . . "

"Me and who else?" Poppy scoffed. "Yes, he did write. A couple of letters were forwarded to me in the Middle East, but I returned them unopened. I wanted to make a completely fresh start."

Jill shook her head, frowning, and Poppy experienced the first pangs of uncertainty. Should she have given Miles the benefit of the doubt and heard what he had to say? It was a disquieting thought and she went to bed with her lovely eyes clouded with indecision.

Despite her troubled frame of mind, Poppy slept well and woke determined not to let the prospect of Miles' occasional presence in Foxbridge make any difference to her life.

After all, she reasoned as she wriggled into her oldest jeans and a red jumper which Jill had put out for jumble, there was nothing he could do radically to alter her life.

She had heard Jill leave the flat early; a glance in the hall cupboard confirmed that her wellies were gone. Poppy grinned. Jill was heavily into conservation and spent a lot of her spare time knee-deep in mud, weeding ponds and ditches, and generally making the world a safer place for newts and frogs.

Poppy ate three slices of toast and honey, drank two cups of tea and then sat back, luxuriating in the sheer indulgence of having nothing to do and all day in which to do it.

After washing up, she decided to clean their elderly, mud encrusted estate car. It was one of the business's vital assets and should not be neglected. Poppy pulled on her bright yellow waterproof jacket and boots and went out to the small cobbled courtyard at the side of the shop.

"Don't you worry," she said, giving the filthy vehicle a friendly pat on the roof. "I'll soon have you looking beautiful again."

She plied the hose enthusiastically, sloughing chunks of gritty mud from the tyres and lower bodywork. Spongefuls of soapy water came next and, after a final rinse, the car emerged gleaming from its bath.

Large pools of frothy water had gathered on the uneven surface of the yard and Poppy impulsively went into her Gene Kelly routine, shuffling about in the puddles and kicking up sprays of water.

"I'm si-i-i-inging in the rain . . . "

A slow handclap halted her and she

knew, without turning around, that it was Miles. Only he could make applause sound ominous. She faced him and they both looked instinctively at the swishing hose she still held in her hand. Oh, the temptation! But it would be tantamount to poking a stick at an enraged rattlesnake.

Regretfully turning off the tap, Poppy threw the hose aside and pushed her dark hair out of her eyes, unconsciously adding another smudge to those already decorating her face.

"Good morning, Miles," she said with a wide, welcoming smile, hoping to throw him off-balance.

It worked. He looked startled, even more so when Poppy tossed him a wad of cleaning rags. "Here, don't just stand there like an ornament; make yourself useful and help me wax the car."

Miles distastefully dropped the grimy bundle. He was wearing a pale suede jacket which must cost him a fortune in dry-cleaning bills.

"You're all dressed up for a Sunday morning in the country," Poppy observed chummily, elated at apparently having found a way of rendering him speechless. "Special occasion?"

At last he found his voice. "Yes, I've come a-wooing."

"A-what-ing?"

"A-wooing," he repeated. "Our parents would have called it courting. I'm not sure of the current idiom. I want us to get together again."

The yard whirled about her and she sat down on the car bonnet with a thump. "You are joking, of course?"

He shrugged. "Partly, although I find the word 'joke' tasteless in this context."

"I find the whole suggestion tasteless," Poppy snapped.

"True, but then tasteful isn't the first word that springs to mind when I think back over certain aspects of our relationship."

"I'm glad you admit it," Poppy said. "The first word that springs to my mind is stupendously horrific."

"That's two words," Miles corrected her.

"Don't be pedantic." They narrowed their eyes at each other, then Poppy turned aside and said to nobody in particular, "This is ludicrous! Why am I standing here, arguing the finer points of the English language with somebody I'd hoped never to see again, let alone speak to?"

"Now you're splitting infinitives," he said waspishly.

"Oh!" Poppy aimed an exasperated kick at the nearest tyre and then, realising how childish she must look, swung back to face Miles. "Look, suppose you say your piece and go — please?"

"Very well." He folded his arms and looked at her steadily. "I am not, by any stretch of the imagination, what could be called a mother's boy, but there are occasions when I feel that I should . . . "

"Indulge her?"

"If you like. I prefer to think of it as putting her interests before my own. She is a very sick woman. She has, for reasons which entirely escape me, become fond of you and it would please her if we appeared to get on better than we do."

"How much better?" Poppy asked faintly.

"Very much better, although she's

quite resigned to the fact that you have someone else."

"Yes. Gordon," Poppy said, clutching at her one frail straw. "Gordon Field. I can't ditch him to play out some silly charade with you — even if I wanted to, which I don't."

"He seems to be a reasonable sort. I got on well with him when I was negotiating for the cottage. Just tell him the truth."

The truth! What was the truth? It was slowly sinking in the quagmire of Poppy's evasions and Miles' half-baked suggestions.

"No, I'm sorry," she said decisively. "The whole thing is too silly. I wouldn't remember how to behave with who."

"Whom," he murmured.

"Oh, shut up!" she shrieked, her temper finally snapping. "How dare you stand there lecturing me as though I were a twelve-year-old?"

"Perhaps because you look like one; your hands and face are filthy." He gave her an unexpected smile of genuine amusement and Poppy took an alarmed step backwards.

"Go away."

"Be reasonable, Poppy. All I'm asking is for you to be sociable; come to dinner or tea occasionally. We'd just have to smile at each other and look as though we enjoy each others' company."

"Fat chance!" Poppy snorted. "If you want acting of that calibre, you'd better send for Meryl Streep! It's beyond my capabilities."

Miles gave a deep sigh. "Very well. Let me put it this way. You have two options: you can spend a few hours of your time indulging in a harmless deception to please Bea, or you can spend the summer looking over your shoulder to see if I'm there, waiting to pounce."

"That's blackmail," Poppy gasped.

"I prefer to call it payment of a debt. You owe me, Poppy. I could have suffered a serious setback in my career because of you."

"What about my career?" she pointed out. "I gave it up completely just to get away from you."

He shrugged. "That was your decision. Personally, I think it was a little drastic.

Good grief, Abu Dhabi! Anyway, this is all beside the point. I'd like you to come to tea at the cottage this afternoon."

Poppy fluttered her lashes at him. "Say please."

"Please."

"No, thank you." She turned away, picked up the bottle of wax and poured a small puddle of it on the car's roof. Miles watched in silence as she methodically spread it over the paintwork. She was acutely aware of him lounging against the gatepost, watching her, and she wished, irrationally, that she didn't present quite such a disreputable picture. She had no wish to impress him but she had the sneaky feeling that, beneath his slightly menacing exterior, he was laughing at her.

This was confirmed when he straightened to leave and, half turning back, said, "Are you going to marry this Gordon person?"

"Why not?" she prevaricated.

"No reason except — " he snorted with laughter — "has it occurred to you that you'll have to go through life calling yourself Mrs Poppy Field?"

4

SEVERAL hours later, Poppy began to see the funny side of the encounter. As she perched on the laundry basket in the bathroom, while Jill wallowed in a much-needed hot tub, she joined in her friend's giggles.

"Miles was right," Poppy choked. "Even if Gordon was the hunkiest, most eligible man in the world, I'd make him change his name before I married him."

"I hope you know what you're doing, love," Jill said. "If Miles is as unprincipled as you say he is, he could make things very awkward for you if you don't fall in with his wishes."

Poppy shrugged. "What could he possibly do to upset me? As far as Miles Hatherford is concerned, I'm shockproof."

But after four uneventful days, she discovered how wrong she was.

* * *

Poppy was woken on Friday morning by the shrill ringing of the phone in the kitchen. She rolled over, looked at the bedside clock and groaned; ten to seven.

"Are you expecting a call?" said Jill's sleep-muffled voice from down the hall.

"Not at this ungodly hour. Let's leave it. If it's urgent, they'll ring back."

They did, five minutes later.

"I'll get it," Jill yelled. "I'm wide awake now, anyway."

Poppy couldn't hear the muffled conversation but after a couple of minutes she heard Jill slam down the receiver and fill the kettle. Pulling on her dressing gown, Poppy joined her friend.

"What was all that about?" she asked, taking in Jill's flushed cheeks. "Golly, it's a bit early for the weirdos to be up and about."

"It was a weirdo all right, but not the usual sort. This one was convinced that we wanted to sell the car. He said there's an advertisement in the local paper with our phone number."

"It must be a misprint. Well, we can soon check."

Poppy went down and collected the Foxbridge Gazette from where it was lying on the side door mat. She leafed through it as she returned upstairs, running her eyes down the Cars For Sale column.

"Yes, here it is." She spread the newspaper on the kitchen table and read aloud, "'Volvo estate. Eight years old but good condition. Blue with beige upholstery. £50. Ring 7902.' Well, it's our car and phone number, but fifty pounds? That's ludicrous! Oh no!"

She snatched up the phone. "Hello? Yes? No, there's been a mistake. Yes, this is that number, but we aren't selling our car. Well, there's no need to be like that. Goodbye!"

She sat down and shook cereal into her bowl. "This is ghastly. The phone's going to ring and ring . . . "

After the eighth call had interrupted breakfast, they decided to leave the phone off the hook until they opened the shop at nine. As soon as the receiver was replaced, the phone shrilled into life and Poppy clutched her head, miming an anguished scream. "Leave it off the hook," Jill advised. "It won't hurt for one day. We'd have to do without it if there was a fault on the line."

"But I don't see why we should have to," Poppy argued. "And what about our own ad, for the shop? We usually get a few enquiries when that appears."

Jill switched on the lights and unlocked the door. "Leave it on then. I'll deal with the calls if you'll go and find out what went wrong at the Gazette. Have a word with Tony. He rather fancies you. It won't stop the blasted phone ringing, but at least we might find out how the mistake happened."

Tony Barton was the owner and editor of Foxbridge's small independent weekly newspaper. He had clocked up forty years, one divorce and countless broken hearts among the local female population, all of which rendered Poppy impervious to his particular brand of laconic charm. Nonetheless, as she sat in his cluttered office, pouring out her tale of woe, she couldn't resist returning his impish grin.

"It sounds horrendous," he commented.

"Tell you what, I'll take you out to lunch to sooth your shattered nerves. No?" He tried to look hurt as Poppy laughed and shook her head. "Oh well, I'll go and see if I can find out how the mistake happened."

He was back within a couple of minutes. "It's a mystery," he announced. "The ad was typed, unsigned, and shoved through the door in a plain envelope."

"Wasn't there a cheque with it for payment?" Poppy asked.

He shook his head. "Cash. The trouble is I've got a new girl handling the small ads. She didn't realise there was anything fishy about it."

"So it was a hoax?"

"Looks like it, sweetie. Never mind, we'll turn it to your advantage. I'll do a piece about it in next week's edition — you know, from a humorous point of view. I'll come down and get a picture of you and Jill. It'll be nice to have some glamour in the paper and it will be a bit of free publicity to you."

Poppy left the Gazette office, rejoicing that things had turned out better than expected. "How many more calls have there been?" she asked after telling Jill the good news.

"I stopped counting when it reached double figures," Jill sighed. "Two were genuine calls. Mrs Tomlinson wanted to know if we've found a chair to go with her Chippendale desk and there was a personal call for you."

"Oh?" Poppy said cautiously. "Who was it?"

"Mr — do call me Miles — Hatherford." Jill fanned herself with mock rapture. "You're right, Poppy. The man's a menace. I found myself telling him all about the trouble we're having and . . ."

"Miles! It was Miles who placed the ad. It must have been."

"Of course. And he was so sympathetic," Jill said indignantly. "Ooh, I do feel silly. There I was, waffling on, and he was making soothing noises. I'll bet he was really rolling about on the floor, laughing. Do you want to get that?"

Poppy snatched up the phone. "Yes?"

"Sold the car yet, Poppy?" Miles purred.

Poppy fought back the impulse to

scream at him that he was a childish idiot. Instead, she purred, "Miles. I've been meaning to ring and thank you but I threw your number out years ago."

"Thank me?" he said guardedly.

"Yes. I guessed it was you who put the ad in the paper. Of course, the calls are a bit of a nuisance but — " she forced a light laugh — "we're going to get some lovely free publicity out of it. Tony Barton — he's the editor of the Gazette — is a close friend of mine and he's going to do a story about how two poor hard-working girls were the victim of a childish practical joke."

There was a long pause and then Miles said, "You can't prove anything. If your friend prints my name, I'll sue him."

"He wouldn't dream of it," Poppy said. "I haven't told him. But don't pull another stunt like that, will you? I'm quite capable of retaliating, and you have a great deal more to lose than me."

She rang off without waiting for a reply, and grinned at Jill. "I don't think we'll be hearing from him again."

"Pity," Jill murmured. "Talking to him

72

is a bit like being massaged with a mink glove. Incidentally, you should watch this habit of claiming intimate friendship with every male acquaintance. It might trickle back to them and they'll get the wrong idea, especially Tony."

"Rubbish," Poppy said airily, elated at how easily she had dealt with Miles. "Do you know, I honestly believe that I've got him out of my hair at last."

They put a message deterring prospective car-buyers on the answering machine, and the rest of the day passed in comparative peace. At ten past five, as Jill counted the takings and Poppy made a note of the few useful calls which had accumulated on the machine, Miles mother came dashing in.

"Oh, my dears, I'm so glad I've caught you before you close," she laughingly gasped, sinking into a chair. "My god-daughter is visiting me on Sunday and I've remembered that it's her birthday next week. She's well past the record token stage and I couldn't think what to get her, then I remembered she collects mice — you know, in pottery or glass or ivory. Do you have anything suitable?"

"I'm not sure," Poppy said, looking around the shop. "Jill, you'd know better than me. Do we have any mice?"

Her friend looked up. "Golly, I hope not! I've nothing against them in the wild but I'd hate to have them on the premises."

Beatrice laughed. "No, I mean the ornamental variety. Look, I'll come back in the morning when you've had a chance to think about it. Oh . . . !" She gasped and clutched at her ribs.

"Glass of water — quickly!" Poppy said to Jill, fear sharpening her voice, as she remembered that Beatrice had a weak heart. She knelt beside the older woman, who was doubled up, ashen-faced, in her chair. After a moment's hesitation, she opened the black leather handbag, which had slipped to the floor. A bottle of tiny white pills was tucked into the side pocket. Poppy carefully read the instructions on the label, shook one out and took the glass of water from Jill.

"Here you are," she gently coaxed. "Down the hatch."

Within ten minutes, Beatrice, although still pale, was her perky self again. "Thank goodness there's always somebody sensible around when I have an attack."

"You should take things easier," Poppy urged with genuine concern. "The way you rush around would send anybody's heart into a tizzy. Now, is there anything else we can get you? A cup of tea, perhaps?"

"No, thank you. I've been quite enough trouble for one day. I'll just sit here for another couple of minutes and then be dashing along."

"You're not dashing anywhere, Mrs Hatherford," Poppy said firmly. "I'll drive you home. And you must call your doctor."

"And you must call me Bea," Miles' mother insisted. "Please. It makes me feel just a little nearer your age. Even Miles calls me Bea, haven't you noticed? Oh, good heavens, he's arriving at seven for the weekend. I must get back and start preparing dinner."

Poppy had always admired the thatched-roofed prettiness of Keeper's Cottage, but this was the first time she had been inside. She looked appreciatively at the sitting-room into which Beatrice led her and smiled with pleasure.

"If I'd known how super all our furniture was going to look, I'd have doubled the prices," she joked. "Now, point me towards the kitchen and I'll make you some tea. And I'm sure Miles will be able to prepare dinner for you."

He had, Poppy recalled as she made tea, been a dab hand at cooking. A picture of him in a striped butcher's apron rose unbidden in her mind . . .

"I've come to see how you're getting along," Beatrice's voice said behind her. "My dear, why so pensive?"

Poppy pulled herself together and smiled. "No reason. I've had a funny sort of day, that's all."

"Funny amusing, I hope, not funny peculiar. Come and sit down and tell me all about it."

After pouring the tea, Poppy gave Beatrice a heavily censored account of the car that wasn't for sale. As she relived their hair-tearing exasperation, Poppy saw the farcical side of the incident and they were both laughing so much that they didn't hear Miles' key in the lock. He stopped dead at the sight of his mother's visitor, and Poppy's eyes widened with apprehension.

"Miles!" Beatrice exclaimed. "You're early. How nice. I must start dinner."

"I don't think you should attempt any cooking tonight," Poppy said easily. "You still look rather pale."

Miles strode across the room and kissed his mother. "Have you had another attack, Bea. Honestly, you've been warned time and time again about overdoing it."

Beatrice dismissed his concern with an airy wave. "It was nothing. I came over rather faint and Poppy kindly drove me home." She turned to Poppy and explained, "I have to make light of it, or they've threatened me with another operation."

"All the more reason to slow down," Poppy said with concern.

Beatrice clicked her tongue with impatience. "If I can't do things at my own pace, I might as well throw in the towel completely." Then her bravado faded and she smiled apologetically at her son. "Would you mind, darling? There's some steak in the fridge."

"Of course not. Perhaps Poppy would care to share it with us?"

His eyes were pleading rather than threatening and Poppy reluctantly nodded. "I'll give you a hand."

In the kitchen, Miles muttered, "What happened?"

"She dashed into the shop to buy a gift for somebody and almost collapsed. I found some pills in her bag, got one of them down her and then brought her home."

"I'm very grateful. Thank you."

"She shouldn't be left alone," Poppy said, concern for Beatrice overriding her reluctance to speak to Miles. "Why didn't you let her go on living in town where you could keep an eye on her?"

"Are you blaming me?" he said angrily. "It was even worse in London. She loves shopping and going to the theatre; she had a social life which would have exhausted a person half her age. There was a huge house and garden . . . I couldn't be behind her every minute of the day. What would you have done?" He slapped the steak on the pan and put it under the glowing grill. "Do you want to make the salad dressing? It was one of your specialities, as I remember."

Poppy raised her eyebrows, surprised that he could recall something so insignificant. He had dated scores of women, all of whom must have had a variety of talents. He must have an amazing mental filing system.

"Why did you pick this particular property?" she asked casually.

"You mean why Foxbridge?" He raised a sardonic eyebrow and Poppy concentrated on whisking the olive oil into the dressing. "Bea saw the cottage advertised in Country Life and refused to move unless it was to come here. If I'd known you were back, living here, I'd have tried harder to divert her somewhere else."

"If you find my presence so obnoxious, why do you keep pestering me?" Poppy snapped.

"I've explained all that; it's to keep Bea happy. And now you've seen for yourself why I try and humour her little whims. If she doesn't slow down . . ."

He ran his fingers through his dark hair and Poppy felt a sudden, unexpected wave of sympathy for him.

"Look," she said awkwardly. "I'm not promising anything, but I'll do what I can — for Bea's sake, you understand. I've become very fond of her."

"Would you, Poppy?" Miles looked relieved. "She does seem to take notice of what you say. If I'd suggested cooking the meal tonight, she'd have hit the roof. Perhaps you could persuade her that getting in a home help isn't a sign that's she's got one foot in the grave."

Poppy gave a cynical grin. "For somebody with your experience, you don't know much about female psychology. Your mother's barely in her sixties. Try hiring somebody young and calling her the au pair. Home help, indeed!"

Dinner was a curious meal. Poppy, a normally truthful girl, found that she had to think very carefully before committing herself to any verbal statement. When Miles made a casual reference to his secretary, Poppy had actually opened her mouth to ask, "And how is the ghastly Sylvia?" before remembering that she wasn't supposed to know anything about his life in London.

Consequently she became quieter and quieter until Beatrice asked, "Are you all right, Poppy? You've gone all pensive again. I suppose you're still shattered from those tiresome phone calls. Miles, the most extraordinary thing happened to Poppy and Jill today. Somebody played the silliest trick on them . . . "

Beatrice launched into an account of the phony advertisement while Poppy concentrated on her chocolate mousse, her sharp ears listening for any false notes in Miles' sympathetic responses. Suddenly her sense of the absurd got the better of her and she felt a hysterical giggle start to bubble in her throat.

"I'll make the coffee," she mumbled, and escaped to the kitchen.

When Miles came to see if she could find everything, he took one look at her as she stood shaking with laughter, one hand clamped over her mouth to muffle any sound, and began to laugh himself.

"Well, I expected all kinds of reactions from you but nothing like this," he said.

"I wasn't so amused at seven o'clock this morning, and neither was Jill. Even

81

if you can't bring yourself to give me an apology, I think she deserves one. She's probably still taking calls. I must go and relieve her when I've had my coffee."

"No, please stay."

Poppy looked pointedly down at Miles' hand on her wrist and he quickly removed it. Then, as their eyes met, Poppy's laughter was replaced by apprehension.

"Please, Miles," she whispered, "don't make my life miserable again."

His long lashes hid his expression. "What makes you think you had the sole concession on misery?"

He swiftly loaded the coffee things on to a tray and headed for the sitting room, leaving Poppy staring after him with a puzzled frown. What was that all about? Surely he wasn't suggesting that her flight from him two years ago had caused him pain?

Beatrice was her usual exuberant self as she poured the coffee. "What do you do for entertainment around here, Poppy?"

Poppy hesitated, reluctant to discuss her own mad round of reading, watching TV and going out for the occasional drink with her small circle of friends.

82

"There isn't much to do," she apologised, "so the locals drive to one of the larger towns or to London when they want a decent night out. Apart from that — " she laughed and lapsed into the local accent — "we country folk make our own amusements."

Miles grinned. "I don't somehow see you weaving corn dollies or doing country dancing."

"Just wait until May Day," she retaliated. "Country dancing is practically compulsory. There's a fete on the common, with sideshows and morris dancers and fancy dress competitions for the children. You either love it or hate it."

"It sounds great fun," Beatrice exclaimed.

"I take it from Poppy's jaundiced tone that she doesn't care greatly for cavorting on the common," Miles said.

Poppy shrugged. "It's OK, but the novelty wears a bit thin when you've cavorted as many times as I have. I was May Queen when I was sixteen. I wore a hideous, frilly white frock, which I thought was wonderful at the time, a crown of wilting flowers, and had the most terrifying ride in the ceremonial hay cart."

"Why terrifying," Beatrice asked, highly diverted.

"The old shire horse who usually pulled the cart was unwell and the only last minute replacement that could be found was one of Colonel Smithson's retired hunters. It was a darn sight too frisky for my liking — I thought I was going to end up rocketing through town, scattering hay and droopy flowers as I went."

They all laughed and Miles said, "You never told me about that."

"Er — no," Poppy prevaricated, conscious of his mother's enquiring look. "It's not the kind of thing you tell a complete stranger."

Miles pulled a face and Poppy hoped that it had brought home to him how difficult it was going to be to prevent Beatrice discovering the truth.

She thought it an appropriate moment to escape and, looking at her watch, said, "It's nearly eight! I must go. Jill wants to use the car this evening."

"Oh no." Beatrice looked disconsolate.

"I was so enjoying your company. You will come again, won't you?"

"I — er — yes, of course. I'd love to. During the week, perhaps?"

When Miles was safely tucked away in London. His presence was proving too distracting for Poppy's peace of mind.

Beatrice smiled. "That would be lovely. Perhaps Jill would like to come as well. Or your young man?"

"My . . . ?" Poppy went blank for a second. "Oh, my young man! Gordon! I don't know. He's pretty busy at this time of year. And he's very involved with the cricket team."

Conscious of Miles' sceptical gaze, Poppy said her farewells and drove home as though pursued by demons.

5

"NOW let me see if I've got this right," Jill said with an air of calm patience which Poppy suspected was bordering on sarcasm. "To keep Beatrice happy, you're going to revive your romance with Miles . . . "

"No, no! She didn't know anything about it in the first place, and we're only going to pretend."

"OK. You're going to pretend to have a romance with Miles, but first you've got to appear, as far as Beatrice is concerned, to get rid of Gordon. But for Miles' benefit you're going to go on pretending to be besotted with Gordon, right?"

"Right," Poppy agreed, screwing up her face with doubt.

"But you aren't even going out with Gordon," Jill objected, "or are you planning on encouraging his attentions just to keep Miles at bay?"

"Good heavens, no! That would be dishonest," Poppy said, shocked.

Jill screeched with laughter. "What's the rest, if not dishonest?"

"A harmless subterfuge to keep Beatrice happy. She's far more fragile than she looks." Poppy's bright face saddened.

It was Sunday morning. The girls were seated on opposite sides of the kitchen table while Jill gave Poppy a long overdue manicure. Jill had trained as a beautician and had worked at it for four years before cheerfully giving it up to run the antique shop. Her current mission was to try and arouse Poppy's enthusiasm for the sudden, albeit unwelcome, upswing in her social life.

She pushed a tray bearing a selection of her own nail polish across the table. "Here, pick a colour."

Poppy looked through the collection and wrinkled her nose. "I gave up this sort of thing ages ago; it attracts the wrong type of men. Ugh, I think I'll give Sexpot Scarlet a miss. How about Delicate Rose? That sounds more like me."

They grinned companionably at one another. Despite her grumbles, Poppy was quite enjoying herself. Besides, if, as

87

seemed likely, she was going to see more of Miles, she wanted to impress him. Not for the usual male-female reasons — heaven forbid — but simply to show him that she was continuing to function as a desirable woman and maybe bring home to him exactly what he had thrown away.

"Face next," Jill ordered.

Poppy groaned. "Do I really need make-up?"

"No," Jill said, looking enviously at Poppy's naturally beautiful colouring, her brows and lashes etched darkly against her rosy tan. "But I'll do it anyway, just to see how it looks."

"Perhaps if I go around covered in a thick layers of paint, Beatrice will decide that I'm totally unsuitable for her precious son," Poppy mumbled hopefully through the thick cleansing gel which Jill was spreading over her face. "Yum, yum, mint! Are you sure we shouldn't be having this with the roast lamb?"

After lunch, Jill settled down with the newspaper and Poppy went for a walk. Apart from enjoying walking, she felt that it would be a waste of Jill's efforts to sit around indoors where nobody could see her in all her technicolour glory! Wearing gold cord slacks and a creamy aran pullover, she presented herself for her parents' inspection.

Her father roused himself from his postprandial nap for long enough to enquire if she had been offered a job as a game show hostess, but her mother was more enthusiastic.

"Darling, you look lovely! Not that you need any artificial aids, but it's nice to see you taking an interest in yourself again."

Poppy remained with her parents for another hour and then left to continue her walk. Skirting the two acres that made up her father's market garden, she struck out along the narrow road that would take her clear of town and into the gently rolling countryside.

As she meandered along, deep in thought, Poppy tried reluctantly to analyse her feelings for Miles. It was something she had been postponing because she knew that she wasn't going to like her conclusions.

For two years he had been the object

of her contempt. Heartless, thoughtless, selfish; all were words she automatically associated with him. She had deliberately forgotten that he was also charming, humorous and, in his behaviour towards Beatrice, tender and concerned. She was so lost in thought that she didn't notice the sleek silver car whispering towards her, and she jumped as it passed, the driver lightly tapping the horn to attract her attention. She caught a glimpse of Miles' profile as he slowed fractionally and then drove away again.

Poppy turned and watched the car vanish around a bend, clenching her fists in her pockets and refusing to respond to his wave. The attractive girl lounging in the passenger seat must be Beatrice's god-daughter, the one for whom she had been seeking an ornamental mouse.

The fence which separated the farming land from common ground ended and Poppy left the road, heading into the fields in which she had spent so much of her childhood.

She began to climb, the leather soles of her boots occasionally slipping on the sappy new grass. At the top of the hill she stopped, panting slightly, and seated herself on the stump of a felled oak. The tree itself lay alongside as it had always done, becoming more hollow and weather-beaten with the passing years. There was a certain security in the familiar landscape, timeless yet ever-changing as the light painted different colours and shadows over the solid permanency of the hills and fields.

Poppy took a deep breath and felt some of her tension ebb away as the silence, broken only by the sighing of the wind and the cawing of rooks, enfolded her. Infrequent cars sped silently along the ribbon of road below and Poppy amused herself trying to identify them. One was ominously familiar and she scowled as Miles' luxurious saloon came cruising slowly back along the road.

Her disapproval turned to dismay as he pulled over on to the verge, locked the car and stood, hands on hips, looking up at her.

As he began climbing the hill, Poppy frantically rearranged her features into a reasonable facsimile of polite disinterest. His progress up the steep incline was swift and graceful and, Poppy noted with irritation, did not even alter the tempo of his breathing. He must still be a twice-a-week squash fanatic.

He moved towards the tree stump but, noting Poppy's expression, seated himself on the tree trunk instead. "This is nice."

"It depends on your definition of nice," Poppy said coldly.

"I was referring to the view."

"Of course." There was an awkward pause which Poppy filled with, "Shouldn't you be helping Bea entertain her guest?"

"Sarah? I did my duty in collecting her from the station. Ten minutes in her company strains even my boredom threshold which, as you might recall, isn't especially low."

"What's wrong with her?" Poppy asked, naturally curious as to why any man would shun the company of an attractive woman.

As if he had read he mind, Miles said, "Not every man is impressed by looks even when, as in Sarah's case, it's accompanied by brains. There are other things."

"Such as?" Poppy couldn't help asking.

"Let's see. A sense of humour. Sarah's never managed to make me laugh in all the years I've known her — at least, not intentionally. Consideration for other people. Sarah's only visiting Bea out of a sense of duty and a vague hope that she might inherit her jewellery."

He stopped ticking Sarah's deficiencies off on his fingers and gave Poppy a sardonic smile. "It's rather late for you to be concerning yourself with my preferences, isn't it? It's a pity you weren't so concerned two years ago."

Poppy's eyes widened. "I wasn't concerned! What about you?"

"Me?" If she hadn't known he was the world's greatest con artist, Poppy would have sworn that the bewilderment in his blue eyes was genuine. "How can you possibly blame me for what happened?"

She slid off the tree stump. "If you don't know, there's no point in trying to explain. Besides, I'd rather not go over it again."

Miles followed her as she turned and

walked away. "How can we go over something we never discussed in the first place?" Poppy quickened her pace and he did likewise. "That's right, run away. That's your solution to everything."

"Not everything," she called over her shoulder, "just an unprincipled swine like you."

"Swine, me? If I'm a swine, you're a self-centred vixen."

Poppy began to run. They'd descended to childish name-calling; another few moments would see them reduced to poking their tongues out at each other. A swift mental picture of them doing just that flashed across her mind and she began to giggle. Her breath hiccuped in her throat and a stitch began to niggle in her side. She stopped, leaning against a tree to regain her breath, and Miles caught up with her.

"Why are you sniggering like a silly kid?"

"Because that's how we're both behaving" she spluttered.

He grinned. "You are the most exasperating creature. I suppose that's why we never had any serious arguments.

You always made me laugh before I could lose my temper."

'I bet you weren't laughing when Sir William walked in and caught you groping Sylvia,' Poppy speculated to herself.

"Well, I'm glad I'm good for something," she said with forced brightness. She glanced around, seeking a fresh topic of conversation. "Oh, we're in Bluebell Wood."

"That's an original choice of name," Miles said, looking at the mass of azure flowers. "Judging by the squashed patches of grass, it's the sylvan equivalent of Lover's Lane. Do you and Gordon ever come and flatten the flowers?"

"Certainly not!" she retorted, before remembering that it wouldn't be such a strange thing, if she and Gordon really were lovers. "Let's face it, it's not very comfortable here."

"How very unromantic. You used to be more adventurous."

"Why do you keep harking back to the past?" Poppy complained. "I don't know about you, but I'm very different from the person I was two years ago."

Miles feigned shock. "You mean you've lost your lovable little habit of trying to get people fired?"

"I didn't do that on purpose! Nor would I dream of putting childish advertisements in the paper."

He tried to brazen it out. "I won't apologise because it had the desired effect."

"I'm friendly with your mother because I like her, not because of your pathetic attempts to intimidate me."

A light spring rain began to fall, pattering softly on the leaves.

"And I'm only going so far with your scheme. We'll pretend to be friends, but nothing more."

Miles looked speculatively at Poppy, her dark hair hanging in a glossy tangle about her shoulders, her topaz eyes wide and vulnerable. "We needn't pretend."

"Thank heaven for that," Poppy breathed, thinking she had been reprieved.

"You misunderstand me," he purred. "I mean that we could play it for real. You're even lovelier now than when we first met. I wouldn't find it too difficult to fall for you all over again."

"I'm sure you wouldn't!" Poppy raged, incensed by his suggestion, but even angrier with herself because her pulse was racing at the vivid pictures conjured up by his words. "From what I can gather, you never were too fussy, but I most definitely am. Honestly, how could you . . . ?"

"Poppy," he interrupted quietly, "you're making too much noise. A simple yes or no would have done. The way you're going on makes me wonder if you're trying to convince yourself, as well as me, that it's not a good idea."

Poppy had forgotten Miles' unnerving ability to read what was going on behind her transparent face. She swallowed hard to banish the sudden dryness from her throat. He was so close that she could smell his cologne, and she edged around the tree against which she was leaning. But he followed her, effectively stopping her progress by placing his hands on either side of her shoulders. She read amusement in his brilliant blue eyes, and detested him for the enjoyment he must be getting out of his revenge.

But his voice was tender when he spoke.

"You should use rainproof warpaint; your mascara is starting to run." He lightly ran the knuckle of his forefinger under her lower lashes and showed her the resulting smudge. "See? Why are you wearing all that junk anyway? I much prefer you without it."

"I beg your pardon. I hadn't realised I was supposed to take your fads and fancies into consideration," Poppy muttered, trying to summon up some defiance to dispel the delicious lassitude that was stealing over her as his lips approached hers. She forced herself to think of her last glimpse of him, before her flight abroad two years ago, as he stood in his office allowing Sylvia do her impersonation of poison ivy around him. It worked and she wrenched herself away. "You've got a nerve!"

He sighed. "Oh, Poppy, whatever's happened to us? We were always able to talk things over until . . . "

"Until you pushed your luck and mentioned marriage. Why did you bother, Miles? Thinking back, it must have been the most halfhearted proposal in the world."

He shrugged. "I didn't want to frighten you off. You were so absorbed in your job that I thought, if I tried to pin you down . . . We could have had one of those open-ended affairs but I didn't want that. I wanted a wife, not a mistress."

No, because he had enough of those. Poppy narrowed her eyes at him. "Oh, I get it. You wanted an unpaid housekeeper; somebody to entertain your business friends. A docile little woman who would sit around your showpiece home while you" — she gulped — "worked late or went on trips abroad."

The rain had ceased to be a friendly shower; it lashed down, icy and malicious, but neither Poppy nor Miles noticed.

"How can you say that?" he protested. "Heavens above, don't you know anything about me?"

"I know everything about you, Miles. I found out just in time."

"What do you mean?"

Poppy pushed her dripping fringe out of her eyes. "Come off it, Miles, you must have thought I was stupid or something . . . Hell's bells, I'm soaked through. What a way to spend my day off!"

As she turned to leave, Miles grabbed her arm but she shook him off. "I don't trust you any more now than I did two years ago. Get out of my life, Miles, and stay out."

She began to scramble down towards the road, careless of the greyish chalky mud splashing her clothes. Her only thought was to get away from Miles. She could hear him calling her name and knew he was coming after her, but she was more agile, instinctively finding footholds while he slipped and slid down the hillside. Resisting the impulse to run, she set off briskly along the road, her head down against the driving rain. A few moments later she became aware that she was being accompanied by Miles in his car.

"Poppy!" he shouted across to her through the open nearside window. "Get in. You'll get drenched."

Get drenched! She was soaked right through to her undies, which were clinging clammily to her skin. She hurried on, not warranting his suggestion worth a reply.

The car continued to creep along

beside her. "I want to know what you meant, Poppy."

"Go away, I have nothing to say to you — and you're embarrassing me," she called. Several passing cars had slowed down to watch the entertaining spectacle of two angry people — one on foot, one in a car — yelling at one another.

A white Rover with a bright orange stripe along its side had begun taking an interest in the proceedings and Poppy smothered a grin as the police car pulled over in front of Miles, forcing him to stop.

A young constable climbed from the passenger seat. "Is everything all right, miss? Is this man bothering you?"

Poppy squelched over to him. "Yes, he is. He's a kerb crawler."

Well, it was true — up to a point! There was the kerb, and Miles had been crawling along it.

Miles joined them. "Come on, darling, don't be silly." He flashed the policeman an apologetic smile. "We had a bit of a tiff back down the road, and she insisted on walking."

Poppy gave him a blank stare. "What

are you talking about?"

The officer reached for his notebook. "Perhaps you'd care to tell me what he was saying to you, Miss . . . ?"

"James — Poppy James," she said quickly, forestalling Miles' ability to give her name and claim acquaintance with her. "Let's forget it, officer. I'm sure he's harmless. I'm sorry you've been troubled."

To her relief, he put his notebook away and returned her smile. "No trouble, Miss James. Perhaps we can give you a lift home. No? Oh well, you carry on then. I want another few words with this character."

Poppy granted him another melting smile and hurried away, leaving the 'character' in question looking as though he was about to choke with rage. Safely back at the flat, she was incredulous when Jill expressed pity for Miles.

She began to towel Poppy's dripping hair with painful vigour. "He could have been arrested and prosecuted."

"Ouch! Not so hard. I wouldn't have let it go that far. What do you take me for?" Poppy defended herself, huddling deeper into her dressing gown and stifling a sneeze. There, Miles had caused her to catch a chill! "If there had been any chance of the policeman taking action, I'd have backed Miles' story. I can't stand the man but I wouldn't have involved him in a scandal."

"I'm glad to hear it," Jill said primly. "Honestly, Poppy, I don't know what's got into you lately. You and Miles are behaving like a pair of loonies."

"He started it!" Poppy spluttered from the depth of the towel. "He should stop pestering me. I've only been behaving like a loony since the Hatherford clan moved into town."

Jill giggled. "Clan? There's only two of them."

"A small mercy for which I should be grateful," Poppy said gloomily, "but, as far as I'm concerned, that's at least one too many."

6

THE following day Poppy woke with a streaming cold and used it as an excuse not to go out with Gordon when he rang with an invitation to visit the cinema.

"I thought you were supposed to be encouraging him," Jill said as Poppy put down the receiver and reached for a tissue. "Miles is going to think it odd if he never sees you and Gordon together."

"Miles is only here at weekends," Poppy snuffled, "and my excuse was genuine. The way I feel right now I couldn't summon up the energy or enthusiasm to go out with Mel Gibson."

"So if he rings, I'll tell him you're not available?"

"Right — but don't put him off completely."

After lunch Tony Barton arrived, as he had promised, to interview and photograph the girls for the weekend edition of the Gazette.

"Oh heavens," Poppy groaned, looking at her cold-ravaged face in the mirror. "Can't you come back later in the week, Tony? I look as though I'm in the advanced stages of bubonic plague."

"Don't fret, sweetie," he chuckled. "The red nose won't show up on black and white film and, apart from that, you're as ravishing as ever. Has the phone stopped ringing yet?"

"Just about," Jill replied. "There were a couple of calls over the weekend but none today — so far."

"And you've no idea who could have placed the ad?"

"None at all," Jill said before Poppy had a chance to reply.

When Tony had gone, Poppy said reproachfully, "You didn't think I was going to sneak on Miles, did you?"

"No," her friend said doubtfully, "but I was just making sure. Tony wouldn't risk printing Miles name and being sued for libel, but he'd talk and you know how gossip spreads in this town."

"Like a sandstorm in the desert,"

Poppy agreed, "and I'd hate to shatter Beatrice's illusions about her precious son. And speaking of Beatrice, shouldn't one of us pop along and see how she's feeling after her nasty turn? I can't go and risk giving her this cold."

"By process of elimination, that leaves me," Jill said. "Yes, I'd like to see her — and have a look at how our furniture has fitted into the cottage. Do you think I should ring first and make sure that the big bad wolf isn't lurking about? On the other hand, I wouldn't mind if he was. I've only met him once and can scarcely remember what he looks like."

"I wish I could say the same," Poppy muttered darkly.

★ ★ ★

"Keeper's Cottage is gorgeous," Jill declared when she returned from her visit. "I wish I could afford a place like that."

"Find yourself a rich husband," Poppy said cynically. "At least you know where you are if you marry for money."

"Then perhaps you should reconsider

your decision to cold-shoulder Miles," Jill said wickedly. "He seems pretty well-heeled. And speaking of Miles, I'll bet he's having fun today. Bea was telling me he's persuaded her to have an au pair girl. She's not well enough to go traipsing up to town so Miles is interviewing them for her."

"Hell's bells," Poppy said, hoping that the sharp pain under her ribs was the hamburger she's had for lunch and not jealousy. "His outer office must look like the venue for a beauty contest. Sylvia must be tearing her blonde hair out by its black roots. I just hope he's sensible and chooses somebody who's useful as well as ornamental."

Jill chuckled. "You're convinced she'll be ornamental?"

"Blonde, Swedish and not a day over twenty," Poppy predicted.

★ ★ ★

As Poppy discovered on Thursday when she took her turn to visit Beatrice, she was right on only one count about the newcomer to Keeper's Cottage. Astrid was blonde but she came from Denmark and was twenty-two. She was tall, shapely and ravishingly pretty, with big grey eyes and silvery hair which Poppy scanned in vain for telltale dark roots. Extremely bright, she was taking a year's sabbatical from university to perfect her English. She was also, somewhat irritatingly in view of all her other attributes, disarmingly nice.

"I've promised Bea that we'll take Astrid under our wing and introduce her to Foxbridge's social life," Poppy reported back to Jill. "That should take about five minutes. I just hope she's easily amused."

The girls were popular members of the Foxbridge Country Club but never more so than on Saturday night when they entered with Astrid in tow. It was evident from the expressions of the lone males at the bar that they thought Christmas had come early.

Poppy was on her second glass of wine when Miles walked in. She and Gordon were seated slightly apart from the others, pleasantly chatting about trivialities. She was getting used to having Miles turn up unexpectedly and scarcely missed a beat in the conversation when she found herself the recipient of his sardonic blue stare. To her acute annoyance and embarrassment, Gordon beckoned him to join them.

She placed her hand over her glass in a gesture of refusal when he asked what they were drinking and, while Miles was at the bar, Gordon murmured, "It's not like you to be churlish, Poppy."

She shrugged. "Sorry, Gordon, but the man irritates me beyond belief. I'll try harder to be sociable."

When Miles returned with the drinks she forced herself to say pleasantly, "I'm sorry I waited until Thursday to visit Bea but I had an appalling chill at the beginning of the week."

He grinned. "So did I. Wasn't that a coincidence?"

"Remarkable," Poppy agreed, wishing she'd known at the time. It would have made her own snuffles more bearable.

"It was kind of you and Jill to volunteer to take Astrid under your wings. I wouldn't like her to get bored or anything."

Poppy mentally raised her eyebrows.

Why not? Why should Miles be concerned about his mother's au pair's well-being?

"It's no trouble," she said pleasantly. "She's charming and I'm sure she won't be wanting for escorts after tonight." In case that sounded waspish, she added, "It must be a relief for you to know that your mother isn't alone at the cottage when you're not there."

"Absolutely," he agreed. "I think that last attack scared her somewhat — she hasn't been so eager to dash about, but that won't last for long. Still, Astrid's a bright girl, so I'm relying on her to keep Bea happy."

"Quite," Poppy agreed, half relieved, half piqued to think she might now be superfluous to Miles' schemes to brighten Beatrice's life. "So any — er — prior arrangement to keep Bea happy can be cancelled?"

He glanced slyly at her from beneath his thick lashes. "Not at all. Finding Astrid was just a bonus to my original plans."

Gordon, sensing an undercurrent, was watching them curiously, and Poppy sought to divert him. "You must have been pleased when you eventually sold Keeper's Cottage, Gordon? It had been on the market for ages."

"It was just a question of finding the right buyer," he said a trifle pompously, as though Poppy had cast aspersions on his professional abilities. "It was too large to be used as a weekend home and too expensive for an average family with an average income . . ."

Poppy felt her eyes glaze over as Gordon droned on, listing the reasons why the cottage had been difficult to sell, and Miles laughed. "Hold on, if you go on making it sound such a liability, I shall put it straight back on the market."

"Yes, please," Poppy wished fervently.

Her eyes met Miles and he must have read her thoughts because he gave an impudent grin. "Don't fret, Gordon. My mother has become very attached to this part of the world and, I must confess, I'm also beginning to appreciate its rustic charm. London can be very tiresome."

"Are we to take it you are also tired of life?" Jill asked as she joined them in time to catch the end of his remark.

Miles chuckled at her quote. "Dr Johnson rated London too highly." He rose and extended his hand. "It's Miss Squires — Jill — isn't it? I believe I owe you an apology?"

Poppy was filled with admiration as Jill ignored this reference to his practical joke and assumed a blank expression. "For what? You must be confusing me with somebody else."

Gordon, becoming increasingly irritated by the secretive air of his companions, rose to his feet. "Would you care to dance, Poppy?"

They went through the arch into a long room where a five-piece band was playing. As they danced, Poppy found it difficult to concentrate on her partner and found her eyes drawn to where Miles and Jill were seated. They were talking and laughing vivaciously, and Poppy wondered what was so darned funny!

She had always enjoyed Saturday evenings. It was the one night of the week when she made a point of socialising, meeting her undemanding friends for a meal or a couple of drinks. This was the second time Miles had spoiled it for her and she wondered if he was going to make a habit of it.

Perhaps, once his mother was settled in, and the novelty of country life had worn off, he would remain in town at weekends. Meanwhile, all Poppy had to do was keep out of his way — not easy in such a small community — and hope that they could maintain the current level of civility.

When she and Gordon returned to the bar, Poppy noticed that Jill's fair head and Miles' dark one were still close together.

Poppy frowned at Jill and, picking up her bag, said, "I'm going to powder my nose. Coming?"

Jill automatically rose and Miles said to Gordon in exasperation, "Why do women always go to the powder room in gangs. What horrors do they expect to encounter that render them incapable of venturing in there alone?"

Gordon merely looked blank but Poppy stifled a giggle. She had forgotten how much Miles' quirky sense of humour appealed to her.

"What were you and Miles talking about?" she asked Jill casually, running a comb through her shining mane of hair. "You both seemed highly entertained."

"He's an entertaining guy," Jill said. "Nice, too."

Poppy gave an offhand shrug. "Superficially, yes, I suppose he is — until you get to know him. I hope for your sake you don't find him attractive."

Jill grinned mischievously. "As a matter of fact, I do, but only in an impersonal sort of way. I rather like the Albert Memorial but I wouldn't want it stuck in the garden."

"Like a giant gnome," Poppy chuckled, relieved for more reasons than she would care to admit that her friend was impervious to Miles charm. "You didn't answer my question. What was so amusing?"

"I can't remember," Jill said with infuriating vagueness. "Nothing special. Why are you so interested? If I didn't know better, I'd say you were jealous."

Poppy went on combing her already

neat hair, horrified to find that she was indeed jealous. Her horror was not that Miles would hurt her again — she would never allow the situation to develop that far — but that she could still find him attractive enough to regard her friend as a rival.

She became aware that Jill was watching her curiously. "Are you all right, love? I've asked you twice if you're ready."

"Ready for anything," Poppy said. "Absolutely anything."

Then Miles asked her to dance and, as she reluctantly accepted, she wished that her knees were as firm as her convictions. It was a slow, dreamy number and, after a brief struggle during which Poppy clenched her teeth and resisted his efforts to pull her against him, they reached a compromise which was still too close for her peace of mind.

"Stop it!" she hissed. "We only do this sort of thing for your mother's benefit and she's not here tonight." A thought struck her. "You're here, Astrid's here; who's looking after Beatrice?"

"Bea does not need to be looked after; she just needs an occasional restraining hand. She's not a naughty child who has to be watched every minute of the day and night."

"I suppose not," Poppy mumbled, feeling foolish. "Tell her I'll come and see her one evening this week."

"Which evening?" he demanded.

"I don't know. Why?" she snapped, half-suspecting that if she named a particular day she would arrive at Keeper's Cottage and find him there, ready and willing to play the ardent suitor.

"No reason. Good grief, Poppy, you're all teeth and claws these days. Whatever happened to the sweet-natured girl who cried all over my shoulder in the cinema when Bambi's mother died?"

"She grew up," Poppy said, hating to be reminded of the days when they were happy together. "All of a sudden she had her eyes opened to the fact that the real world isn't a Walt Disney fantasy." ·

The dance ended and, wrenching herself from Miles arms, Poppy pushed her way through the crowd and headed for the long, open windows which led to the garden.

The clubhouse was a converted Victorian villa and, as she wandered along the deserted terrace, Poppy glanced into the spacious rooms where members were dining, drinking and dancing. Passing the ballroom, which had been turned into a disco, she paused and watched the frenetic crowd gyrating to the deafening beat.

Astrid was there, her silvery hair changing to purple and green under the strobe lighting. Poppy stood admiring her agility and skill and then noted uneasily that the young Danish girl's partner was Tony Barton. Really, he was old enough to know better. Making a mental note to drop a hint to Astrid about Tony's unsuitability as a dancing partner — or anything else, come to that — Poppy turned and walked straight into Miles.

"You're following me again," she accused him, backing away. "Why are you always following me?"

"Because I'm hoping that, one day, you'll stand still long enough to explain those enigmatic accusations you keep throwing at me. I think we should straighten out a few things, Poppy."

"Like what?" she scoffed.

"Like how we feel about each other?" he suggested.

Poppy found difficulty in replying. Could he honestly be in any doubt about her feelings for him? Surely she had made it plain that she couldn't stand the sight of him? The fact that she herself wasn't entirely convinced was beside the point. It was enough that Miles accepted it.

"The last thing I want to discuss with you is my feelings. I would have thought that if you have any sensitivity, which I very much doubt, you would have got the message by now. Go away, Miles. Leave — me — alone."

She turned and he caught her arm. "You're doing it again — walking away."

Poppy tried to unclamp his fingers from her arm. "Let go of me."

Miles frowned at the note of despair in her voice and slackened his grip without releasing her. "I can't concentrate with all this din. Let's go somewhere quiet."

He pulled her away from the pulsating lights and music into the shadows of a wisteria-covered summer-house. Their footsteps echoed on the wooden floor as they entered and turned to face each other.

"Well, say your piece and let me get back to my friends. They'll be wondering where I am."

"You've forgotten yourself." His voice was mocking. "Don't you mean Gordon will be wondering where you are? Or am I wrong in thinking he's merely a decoy to discourage me?"

Poppy sighed, sick of the pretence. "It didn't take a genius to work that out."

"We're getting to the truth at last."

"Truth? You wouldn't recognise the truth if it jumped up and bit you," Poppy said wearily. "Oh, this is silly. I'm going back inside. I shall freeze, standing out here, wasting time with you."

Her teeth started to chatter, partly from cold, partly as a reaction to Miles proximity. She could barely see him in the darkness, but she could hear his light breathing, and smell the familiar scent of his after-shave. She was so aware of him that she could scarcely breathe.

"You are silly, wandering about out of doors in a flimsy dress. Here, let me warm you up."

Stepping forward, he enclosed her in the circle of his arms. His voice and touch were so gentle that Poppy was beguiled into leaning against him — just for a moment — luxuriating in the illusion that his tenderness was untainted by what she knew him to be.

She gave a deep, shuddering sigh and felt Miles' arms tighten about her. His murmured words were indistinct and, when she enquiringly turned her head, he took it as an opportunity to kiss her. She tried not to respond or panic but she did both. Her lips parted briefly, ecstatically against his before she tried to wrench herself away from him, shaking with the intensity of her mixed emotions.

But he refused to let her go. Without appearing to make any special effort, he imprisoned her against him, stroking her hair and murmuring soothingly, as one would with a frightened kitten.

"Don't fight me, Poppy. Please, darling, I'm sorry for having hurt you. You don't know how much I've missed you."

Poppy stood still, hardly daring to breathe as she listened to the urgency in his voice. Every instinct in her wanted to forgive him, to capitulate and give herself up to the waves of delight that were flooding through her. Perhaps he had changed . . .

Miles turned her face to his and brushed soft kisses over her eyes, cheeks and lips. Poppy leaned against, helpless with desire.

He framed his long fingers around her face, seeking her expression in the dim light. "Poppy, please may we try again? I knew it was wrong for us to be apart the moment I saw you again. I want so much to make you happy, to make both of us happy."

Acquiescence was trembling on her lips when he went on, "I still can't fathom out what it was that I did to make you so angry, but I'm sorry — a thousand times sorry — for whatever it was."

Reality hit Poppy like a douche of icy water. How could he truly be sorry if he didn't know the reason for his oh-so abject apologies?

"Take your hands off me!" she hissed, twisting out of his embrace. "And don't ever, ever try that again. If you're so desperate for female company, try bringing one of your girlfriends with you from London. I'm not interested."

He looked as though he was going to argue but he stepped away from her, saying harshly, "As you wish — for the time being. But you'll see me again."

This sounded so ominous that, as she watched him walk away, Poppy found that she was shivering again — and this time it wasn't with cold. She had hoped that her relationship with Miles was settling into a state of courteous neutrality, but it seemed that he had other ideas.

7

WALKING back to the clubhouse, Poppy shuddered again as she thought of her narrow escape. Miles had been so convincing; he had almost persuaded her that he was sincerely repentant. She found herself reflecting how much easier life would be if she could forget her scruples and accept him as he was, faithless and devious. Because there was no denying that she was still attracted to him.

His threat that she would see him again was no idle one. Instead of leaving, he had resumed his former seat with Jill and Gordon, and Poppy was obliged to rejoin them when she returned. For a moment she and Miles glared at each other in stony silence before she fixed her gaze on the wall and he assumed great interest in the ceiling.

There was a long awkward silence which Jill filled with a commonplace remark about the band. Poppy and Miles remained silent, each too preoccupied to reply, but Gordon, bewildered by the tense atmosphere, seized on it and rambled on at length about the music.

"Who's that man Astrid's been with all evening?" Miles suddenly asked as the blonde girl came into the bar with Tony Barton. "He's a little old to be hanging around with a girl scarcely out of her teens."

"Tony owns the Foxbridge Gazette," Jill said. "Yes, somebody really should have a word with him about cradle snatching."

"The man's a menace," Gordon said pompously. "No woman's safe when he's around."

Poppy fiddled uncomfortably with her glass and wondered if Miles would recall her rash claim to close friendship with Tony.

"You know him, Poppy. Can't you say something to him?"

Poppy's eyes widened, partly with surprise that Miles was still speaking to her, albeit not very civilly. "No, I can't! I'm sorry but it's none of my business — and I don't know him that well."

Miles looked unconvinced and Jill said, "I don't think he's totally unscrupulous, just a bit of a flirt. And Astrid seems to be a sensible girl; she's so pretty she must be used to fending off wolves like him. I wouldn't worry if I were you, Miles."

He shrugged. "I suppose not."

Why was he so concerned, Poppy wondered? Perhaps he had designs on Astrid himself and was piqued because she seemed to prefer Tony's company. She smothered a rueful grin; two failures in one evening; Miles must be losing his knack. Then she took a hasty sip of wine as she recalled the effect he'd had upon her. Miles' knack — whatever it was — was in better shape than ever.

★ ★ ★

"You're jealous!" Jill accused Poppy over breakfast the following morning.

"I am not!" Poppy denied. "I was worried about you. I had a fit when I saw you getting out of Miles' Jag last night. I thought, when I came home early in our car, that Gordon would give you a lift."

"Miles asked me first," Jill said smugly. "I'm a big girl, you know. He was a perfect gentleman but I could have dealt with him had he not been. I don't understand you, Poppy. You're a regular dog-in-a-manger. You don't want him yourself but you have a fit if he so much looks at another woman. You should have seen your face when he asked you to tell Tony to leave Astrid alone."

Poppy's cheeks flamed. "That's not true!"

"And later," Jill went on mischievously, "when Miles and I were saying goodnight, I could practically feel you glaring at us out of the window."

"I wasn't," Poppy gasped. "And you didn't . . . "

"No, of course not," Jill chuckled. "I'm winding you up — not difficult where Miles is concerned. I'm beginning to think that it's a good thing you didn't marry him; the two of you would never have been completely alone together."

"What do you mean?" Poppy demanded, wishing that Jill hadn't mentioned Miles and marriage in the same sentence.

"I mean the old green-eyed monster. It would have been a permanent member of your household. You're never going to have a satisfactory relationship with any man, let alone one as attractive as Miles, until you learn not to see every other woman as a potential rival."

"But it wasn't always like that," Poppy argued. "It never occurred to me to be jealous of anybody until Sylvia Delgarth opened my eyes to what Miles was really like, and shattered my faith in the entire male sex."

"Well, it's about time you did something to restore that faith," Jill said briskly, pouring herself another cup of coffee and spreading the Sunday newspaper out before her on the table, "or you're going to end up a right old sourpuss. I say, look at this. Isn't this Miles' boss?"

She half-turned the paper around and Poppy craned to look. "Yes. What's he been up to to warrant a full-page spread in a scandal sheet? He's supposed to be very strait-laced."

Jill scanned the few column inches surrounding the large photograph of Sir William Macuird, looking rakish in evening dress, and his pretty, elegant wife. "It seems he's had an affair with his secretary and his wife's filing for divorce. It's a wonder any work gets done at Macuird's, with everybody carrying on with everybody else. He doesn't sound very strait-laced to me."

"Why are the papers making such a fuss about it? Divorces among the rich and famous are two a penny."

Jill read on and giggled. "She walked up to him in a posh restaurant and threatened to clobber him with a champagne bottle."

"It isn't funny," Poppy said crossly. "Just wait until you find yourself in the same boat — you'll laugh on the other side of your face."

And with this mixture of metaphors, she stamped off to wash her hair and work on a scheme which would enable her to avoid Miles Hatherford for the rest of her life!

★ ★ ★

On Thursday evening Poppy paid her promised visit to Beatrice Hatherford.

128

"This is nice," Miles' mother greeted her. "I was resigned to a dull evening with the TV. Astrid is good company but I have to let the poor girl off the leash occasionally. She's gone to the cinema with her young man." She gave a wicked chuckle as she led the way into the living room. "I use the term 'young man' loosely; he's really far too old for her but, still, it's none of my business."

"Miles was concerned about Astrid dating this Tony person," she chattered on, handing Poppy a glass of white wine, "but, then, Astrid's father is a friend of Miles' boss, so he feels more than usually responsible for her while she's here."

The conversation turned to the outrageous press coverage of the disintegration of Sir William and Lady Macuird's marriage.

"Poor Ruth," Beatrice sighed. "Such a charming person. We sit on a couple of charity committees together and I know the family quite well. I can't think what's got into Billy, preferring that harridan of a secretary — and others, according to her. Ruth didn't know a thing about any of it, but that's so often the way, isn't it? She used to work for Miles until he arranged for her to be promoted."

"Who? Lady Macuird?" Poppy asked, puzzled.

"No, Sylvia Delgarth, the woman Billy's supposed to be involved with. Apparently she went to Ruth and spilled the beans without turning a hair. I fell out with her several times when she worked for Miles."

"I'm not surprised," Poppy said, too startled by Beatrice's revelation to think what she was saying. "I couldn't stand her either."

She clapped a hand over her mouth but it was too late; the words were out.

Beatrice pounced on Poppy's slip of the tongue. "I knew it! I just knew you were Miles' Poppy! You both gave yourselves away that evening you dined here. Oh, Poppy, why are you going through this absurd pretence of not knowing each other?"

"We didn't know each other terribly well," Poppy evaded, "and it was a long time ago."

"But why pretend you were strangers?" Beatrice persisted.

"I — I don't know. We didn't part on the best of terms and — well, I suppose it was easier to carry on as though we didn't know each other than to have to explain to people."

"Like I'm forcing you to do now," Beatrice said sympathetically. "I'm sorry, Poppy. Here, let me get you another drink."

She got up and bustled about, pouring drinks and fetching some savoury snacks from the kitchen. But when she sat down again, Beatrice said, "I was struck by your unusual name, but thought that it was just a coincidence. What an extraordinary thing! I often wondered what happened," she went on thoughtfully, almost as though she had forgotten that Poppy was seated nearby. "I was convalescing abroad after my first lot of heart surgery, and he used to write me long, lyrical letters about a girl called Poppy and all the plans he had. I was so thrilled that he seemed intent on settling down. Then the letters stopped, quite suddenly, and he was — I don't know — different, quieter when I came home. I could never bring myself to ask what happened."

She lapsed into silence. Poppy stared down at her fingers twisting themselves together in her lap and refused to meet the older woman's eyes. The last person in the world she was going to enlighten about Miles' behaviour was his mother. If Beatrice chose to believe that it was Poppy who had made him unhappy instead of the other way round, then so be it.

At last Beatrice sighed. "I'm sure you and Miles have perfectly good reasons for whatever it was that happened — you're both sensible young people."

Sensible! It was the last word Poppy would have used about her and Miles' behaviour but she nodded agreement.

By sticking firmly to neutral topics and maintaining a relentless cheerfulness, they got through the rest of the evening without further grief. But as she drove away, Beatrice's unexpected kiss still light on her cheek, Poppy felt a wave of misery sweep over her. What a mess! What a ghastly mess!

Ignoring the turning that would take her home, Poppy drove straight on and parked at the top of a hill overlooking

Foxbridge. Getting out of the car, she walked round to the front and perched on the bonnet. She sat there for a long time, looking down at the lights of the little town spread out below her.

A soft breeze rustled the leaves of a nearby oak, and she echoed its sigh as she went over her conversation with Beatrice. There was so much that didn't tally with the neat conclusion Poppy had reached and with which she justified her attitude towards Miles.

It wasn't so odd that Sylvia Delgarth was now secretary to somebody other than Miles — heaven knows she had worked hard enough for her promotion to the Chairman's outer office! — but what had Beatrice meant about Miles' 'long, lyrical letters' and 'all his plans'? How could somebody with a personal life as hectic as his make plans of the kind Beatrice implied?

There was something else worrying Poppy but she couldn't put her fingers on it; something that had struck a chord and then been obscured by the next turn of the conversation.

Shivering, she got back into the car and

headed for home. It would come back to her eventually, when she wasn't even thinking about it; it was just a matter of waiting.

She had to wait only a couple of hours to discover what it was that had been tormenting her. A car cruising past her bedroom window backfired and jerked her awake. As she turned over, Poppy recalled the words which had been bothering her: "She went to Ruth and spilled the beans."

That was it; the curious parallel between her own shattered affair with Miles and Lady Macuird's broken marriage. The ingredients were the same: an unfaithful man, a disillusioned woman — and Sylvia Delgarth, openly admitting her role as the 'other woman'.

Poppy sat up in bed, her heart racing. It was possible that Sylvia was a genuine femme fatale, a woman whose beauty and sex appeal were irresistible to all men, but Poppy doubted it. Perhaps Miles, a bachelor with no ties or responsibilities, might risk an affair with her, but she wasn't so fascinating as to tempt somebody with strong moral views, somebody like Sir William Macuird. So had Sylvia, for obscure, scheming reasons of her own, lied to his wife about her affair with him?

If that was the case — Poppy shuddered with horror as she realised the mistake she might have made — Sylvia could have been lying about Miles. She could have engineered the 'love' scene in his office, knowing that Poppy, always punctual, would arrive in time to witness it!

Poppy hardly slept for the remainder of the night, so confused were her thoughts and emotions. She rose at seven thirty, heavy-eyed and aching with tension.

Jill eyed her with concern. "Are you OK? You look a bit frayed at the edges. You're not coming down with something, are you?"

Poppy mumbled an excuse and Jill went on, "Why not go back to bed for a couple of hours? Sleep it off, whatever it is."

Poppy had already decided to take the morning off and she gratefully seized on Jill's offer. "I won't go back to bed but I would like to get away for a couple of hours. I think I'll drive into Oxford and have a browse round the bookshops."

She flashed Jill a carefree smile and silently begged her pardon for the white lie.

When Jill had gone down to unlock the shop, Poppy bathed and dressed in a new pink silk shirt and white slacks. After making two phone calls, one to directory enquiries, the other to the number she had been seeking, Poppy slipped out of the side door, her mouth dry with nerves. What she was doing was quite crazy but she had to set her mind at rest over whether or not she had done Miles a grave injustice.

Exactly what she would do should she discover she had wronged him hadn't occurred to her, and she deliberately put it out of her mind as she sped along. If she started imagining that the reunion Miles seemed to want was possible, on her terms as well as his, and then discovered that it wasn't, she didn't think she could bear it.

8

THE Macuirds' country house was a Jacobean mansion just outside the pretty Cotswold village of Ashton St. Mary. Poppy had rung to make sure that Lady Macuird was still in residence and would be willing to see her, but she felt a tingle of apprehension as she drew up before the house.

Two Alsation dogs rushed out and tried to surround the car and, as Poppy sat waiting for someone to call them off, she noticed that her hands were trembling. She hadn't attempted to remind Lady Macuird of her identity, simply saying that she had some information about Sir William and relying on the other woman's curiosity to gain an interview.

A slim, dark-haired woman in denim dungarees came round the side of the house and called the dogs to heel. They sat at her feet as Poppy stepped from her car, nervously fiddling with the strap of her bag.

"Miss James?" The woman came forward, her hand outstretched. "I'm Ruth Macuird."

As they shook hands she went on, "As I told you on the phone, if I find out you're another reporter, I'll set the dogs on you."

Poppy managed a wry smile. "Let's wait until you've heard what I want to say."

Ruth Macuird led the way round the house to a wide verandah scattered with cane furniture. Pulling two chairs near the table, she indicated that Poppy should sit down. The gardens were magnificent and Poppy was happy to be distracted by them while her hostess went in search of refreshments. There was an air of peace and permanency about the long lawns and trellised walks, and Poppy could only guess at the wrench it would be for anyone to leave it all behind.

As if to answer Poppy's unspoken question, Ruth Macuird said as she joined her, carrying a tray, "I'll miss this old place dreadfully when I leave but, still, it was my choice." She indicated her dishevelled appearance. "I was packing when you arrived. I've been at it for days. It's not easy to bundle up fifteen years into a few cases. Billy's stayed in town ever since I made it clear that . . . "

She broke off with a sigh and a helpless gesture. There were fine lines of strain about her pretty eyes and her hands shook as she poured the coffee. Poppy felt a wave of sympathy for her.

Ruth said, "Now, let's get on with this chat you were so keen on. You mentioned on the phone that it was something to do with my marriage — what's left of it. Oh, gosh — " a comical look of mock alarm crossed her face — "you're not another one of my husband's girl friends come to confess all, are you?"

Poppy found herself warming to this wry, humorous woman, and even more convinced that Sylvia Delgarth's hair-raising tale about Miles' affairs — at least the one he was supposed to have had with Ruth — was a lie.

"No," she replied "I'm not another Sylvia Delgarth, Lady Macuird."

"You obviously know her, so you'll agree with me when I say thank heaven

139

for that; one of her is more than enough. Do call me Ruth, by the way. I've never cared much for this 'Your Ladyship' business." She gave a bright smile which didn't quite take the sadness from her eyes. "Haven't we met before, Poppy?"

Poppy nodded. "Briefly, a couple of years ago. I used to go around with Miles Hatherford." Her companion still looked puzzled so she added, "We met at a reception. I wore a red dress."

"Of course." Recognition dawned and Ruth frowned. "You're the girl who gave Miles such a hard time. Billy told me all about it. Something about you walking in on Miles and Sylvia and getting the wrong end of the stick. She'd lost her cat or something."

"Lost her cat!" Poppy snorted, not for the first time.

Ruth laughed. "I didn't have her figured for an animal lover, either. Poor Miles, he's such a poppet. You didn't just leave him because of that one silly incident, did you?"

"Not entirely." Poppy flushed at the implied criticism. "I had another reason — I thought it was perfectly reasonable at the time, but now I don't know. I'm becoming more sure by the hour that Sylvia deliberately staged that scene in Miles' office for my benefit, and all the other things. I think she lied to me and — possibly — to you. You see — " she took a deep breath — "Miles and I had more or less decided to get married. I mentioned it to Sylvia in the powder room before the reception. She — she laughed and told me that I was a fool to be taken in by him and that he had a string of girl friends, herself included. I didn't want to believe her but she was so plausible."

There was a long silence. When Poppy had recovered sufficiently to look up, Ruth was staring at her with something like disbelief. "Did my husband pay you to come and tell me this story?"

"No, honestly," Poppy begged. "It's all true. When Beatrice Hatherford told me the details of your — er — upset, it seemed too much like my own experience with Sylvia to be a coincidence. I'm sorry if you think I'm being silly and over imaginative . . . "

"No, no, I'm fascinated, if only by

141

meeting another one of Sylvia's victims. Perhaps you're reading too much into it. Let me get this right. What did Miles say when you confronted him with Sylvia's story?"

Poppy flushed with shame. "I never did. I was going to next day, but when I went to his office and found him and Sylvia locked in what looked like a passionate clinch, I turned and ran. I assumed his conscience would tell him why I left. Did you tell your husband?"

"Yes, I did, in no uncertain terms, but I didn't give him a chance to defend himself and I've refused to speak to him since. I've been beside myself with rage; he's always set himself up as a paragon of virtue." Ruth gave a slightly hysterical giggle. "Why do you suppose she always confronts her victims in powder rooms. Billy and I were celebrating our fifteenth wedding anniversary — it was Sylvia who booked the table — and suddenly there she was, telling me these awful stories about what she and Billy get up to when they were working late."

"And the trips abroad," Poppy reminded her.

"Good heavens, yes," Ruth said in wonderment.

A surge of hope flashed through Poppy. "Oh, Ruth, is it possible that we were tricked into walking out on them — Miles and your husband, I mean?"

Ruth slumped back in her chair, the sparkle dying from her eyes. "We still can't be sure that Sylvia isn't the Jezebel of the executive floor. Perhaps she has been having affairs with Miles and Billy and goodness knows who else. We can't very well go around looking for other disgruntled wives and sweethearts to check their stories for flaws."

What could be a bigger flaw than Sylvia's accusation against Ruth herself? But how could Poppy ask such a personal and insulting question? Oh well, she'd risked humiliation coming here today and it had all gone well so far.

She took a deep breath. "Ruth, I'm going to ask you something you won't like. It was something Sylvia said to me that she wouldn't have included in her little chat with you. Did you influence your husband's decision to promote Miles to the board?"

Ruth stared. "I suppose I did, as far as my husband allows himself to be influenced. Miles has always been one of my favourite young men. What's that got to do with anything?"

Poppy's face flamed with embarrassment. "Well — I mean — was Miles . . . ? Were you and Miles . . . ?" She trailed to a halt, unable to speak her suspicions aloud.

"If you mean was Miles ever my lover, the answer is no, definitely not. Oh, Poppy — " Ruth's eyes gleamed with triumph — "that's the lie we were looking for. It's sent her whole story tumbling like a pack of cards. Miss Delgarth got just a little too clever when she tried to implicate me in her sordid little tales. Thank goodness you had the sense and guts to confront me with it."

"If only I'd done it two years ago," Poppy mourned. "But why? Why did she tell all those lies?"

"Jealousy, I should imagine," Ruth speculated. "She's obviously one of those neurotic women who have little or no life outside their work. They're unable to separate devotion to the job from a crush on the boss. And you must admit that both our men are very attractive."

Poppy felt her elation die away. "I don't think Miles qualifies as being my anything. It's all over between us. I don't love him any more."

"Of course you do," Ruth urged her. "Why else would you risk looking a fool by coming here today?" She took Poppy's hand and gave her a tremulous smile. "Oh, Poppy, I wonder what humble pie tastes like? I think we're both going to find out very soon."

For the rest of the day Poppy agonised over how, when and where she was going to make her long overdue apology to Miles. To confront him with the truth about her lack of trust would be bad enough, but to have to admit that her jealousy had been based solely on the words of somebody else would destroy utterly any tender feelings Miles might still have for her. She now knew that his marriage proposal had been genuine.

Several times Poppy lifted the phone, intending to call Miles at his office, but she knew that the only honourable way of apologising would be to do it face to face. She would have to look into his eyes — they would be like blue ice — and see any remaining trace of affection die.

She decided that her confrontation with him would be the following evening. Beatrice had told her that Miles would be spending the weekend in Foxbridge, so he was bound to turn up at the club.

In the same spirit as condemned men who eat hearty breakfasts, Poppy went out on Saturday morning and brought herself a new outfit; a slinky number in sapphire crushed velvet. She had little hope of impressing Miles but there was no harm in going down with the band playing and all flags flying.

However, he certainly looked impressed when he strolled into the club that night and spotted Poppy standing at the bar with a group of friends. He appeared to have forgotten their angry exchange of words the previous week and smiled wickedly into her eyes as he joined her. The room whirled and Poppy blamed the two vodka and tonics she had drunk in order to get a little Dutch courage inside her before he arrived.

Jill, who knew nothing about the latest

developments, nudged her as if to say, "There, he's yours for the taking."

'If only he was,' Poppy thought wistfully, struck by the irony of the situation. The revelation which had restored Miles to her affections was, when she revealed it to him, going to place him totally beyond her grasp. As he turned to order a drink, Poppy took the opportunity to look at him closely.

Suddenly, within the space of thirty-six hours, he had become as dear to her as he had been two years ago, before she had made such a mess of everything. Dearer even, because she now knew how empty her life had been without him.

Miles turned towards her, the remark he had been about to make dying on his lips as he caught the expression of longing in her eyes.

"Poppy," he murmured. "Why are you looking at me like that?"

The band in the next room struck up and their companions drifted away, leaving Miles and Poppy alone. He came closer and repeated his question.

Poppy wrenched her gaze away from his. "Looking at you like what?" she prevaricated. "You're imagining things."

"No, I'm not," he said. "You were looking at me the way you used to when I thought you loved me — before I did whatever it was that was so awful."

The tender moment passed and his voice took on the sarcastic edge she had recently become used to. "I suppose there's no point in asking you again what it was I did that was so wrong?"

The moment had come! Poppy swallowed and took a deep breath. "I — er. Miles, I have to tell you something. You aren't going to like it but . . . "

A pair of fresh arrivals came and propped up the bar beside them, and Poppy hesitated. An audience was the last thing she wanted. Miles evidently felt the same. With an impatient grunt, he grasped her elbow and towed her outside to where his car was parked. He unlocked the door, thrust her into the passenger seat and then joined her. "OK, Poppy, I'm waiting."

"Very well, Miles, but I'm only telling you because I now know that I was wrong, and I owe you an apology."

"What's happened to make you change you mind?"

"Yesterday I went to see Ruth Macuird and we both decided that we'd made prize idiots of ourselves. Still, it's nice to know that I'm not the only one who jumps to wrong conclusions and makes horrible, stupid mistakes."

Poppy heard Miles fidget impatiently beside her and realised she wasn't making a great deal of sense. She ploughed on, hoping he would refrain from strangling her until she finally got to the point. "If Ruth hadn't gone for her husband with a champagne bottle, it wouldn't have got into the papers and I wouldn't have . . .

"Poppy — " his voice was ominously quiet — "what are you waffling about? Are you never going to tell me what I've waited two years to hear? At this rate it'll be another two years before you get to the point. Start at the beginning, when you left my office and vanished from my life without a word of explanation."

Poppy bit her lip and hoped that Ruth was making a better job of her apology. Perhaps they'd swap notes one day. "I was in love with you, Miles. I even hoped to marry you, but that idea was soon squashed by Sylvia Delgarth."

"Sylvia?" Miles interrupted. "What were you thinking of, telling her our private business?"

It was, in the light of what has transpired, a reasonable question, and Poppy blushed unseen in the darkness. "We met in the powder room before the reception. She started making her usual bitchy remarks — oh, Miles, you should have heard what she used to say to me when you weren't around — and I thought I could shut her up by telling her we were engaged. She countered that by telling me that you and she were lovers."

"What?" The well-sprung car rocked as Miles twisted around to get a better look at Poppy's face. "You're joking!"

"I wish I was. And it wasn't just her. From what she told me you made Casanova sound like a beginner. According to Sylvia . . . "

Miles banged both fists down on the steering wheel and Poppy flinched. "How dare you take Sylvia's word against mine?

150

Come to that, why didn't you give me a chance to defend myself, Poppy? Why didn't you?"

He sounded so despairing that Poppy's stomach contracted with horror. "I was going to," she wailed. "I came to your office the next day and — well, you know what happened. The two things might have been explained separately but together — one seemed to confirm the other. Sylvia knew I was coming and made sure I walked in on what looked like a steamy love scene between you. I didn't know then that she was a jealous neurotic who would do and say anything to drive me away. It was only when I realised that she had pulled the same stunt with the Macuirds that I knew how wrong I'd been."

Miles was silent for a long moment and Poppy held her breath, praying that he would see her point of view.

"I suppose I can see how it must have looked," he admitted, "but it doesn't say much for your trust in me. Still, if she managed to convince Ruth that Sir William was cheating on her after all those years of happy marriage, Sylvia must have a very fancy line in stories — and she must be very believable."

Poppy let out a long sigh of relief as he went on, "I'll have to do some apologising to Sir William myself, for having a troublemaker like Sylvia transferred to his office. I used to think she was conscientious, working until all hours, until the other guys started teasing me about her. I arranged for her to be promoted. I didn't realise she would transfer her obsession for the boss along with her custom-built typing chair."

"So you understand?" Poppy asked anxiously.

"I understand why you walked out, but not why you went to Ruth with your story."

This part wasn't so humiliating and Poppy's voice became more confident. "I read about the problems the Macuirds were having. Beatrice told me some things that weren't in the papers — she mentioned Sylvia — so I put two and two together and went to talk to Ruth. In the light of the evidence, we decided we'd both made dreadful mistakes and that apologies were called for. That's what

I'm doing now — apologising."

There, she'd done it! There was nothing more to say. She turned to scramble out of the car but Miles' hand shot out and grasped her arm. "Hang on! Is that what you call an apology?"

"What more do you want?" she asked wearily. "I'm not going to grovel, even though I was terribly in the wrong."

"I don't want you to grovel — just be a little more gracious. How about 'I'm sorry, Miles'?" he suggested.

Poppy thought about it. Yes, it wasn't too much to ask. "I'm sorry, Miles," she repeated like a naughty child.

"Good." He slid his arm along the back of the seat. "Now, how about 'I love you, Miles'?"

"No!" She flung herself away from him. She was still too vulnerable even to think along those lines. Anyway, how could there be real love without trust?

"Fair enough." To Poppy's relief, Miles sat back and folded his arms. "I think we've made enough progress for one night. At least I've found out what's been eating at you all this time. It's incredible — " he shook his head to emphasise his disbelief — "that jealousy could make Sylvia tell such appalling lies. But you, Poppy, how could you believe her?"

Poppy was grateful for the darkness that hid her humiliation. "She was so plausible, Miles. I was so hurt, I just wanted to hurt you back."

"You certainly did that," Miles muttered. "I've been hurting ever since you walked out without a word of explanation."

"Well, you've had you explanation," Poppy said defensively. "I hope it makes you feel better."

He heaved a deep sigh. "I don't know how it makes me feel. I can't believe you had so little trust in me."

"Stop it!" Poppy begged in agony. "Before we know where we are, we'll be speculating on what might have happened had I not believed Sylvia."

"Exactly. We'd be married and . . . "

"Don't!" Poppy cried, unable to bear the picture he conjured up. "You don't know that for certain. The whole thing might have died a natural death. Let's face it, I wasn't the first girl you dated and I'm sure I wasn't the last."

"I like company," he admitted, "and, yes, I usually had a female companion. But I steer clear of the hearts-and-flowers kind of relationship these days."

The kind that hurts when it goes wrong. The words lay unspoken between them.

"I'm sorry, Miles," she whispered. "I'm so sorry. Is there anything I can do to make amends?"

He took her hand and fiddled with the narrow silver ring she always wore. "We could pick up where we left off."

"No!" Poppy snatched her hand away. "I'm not . . . I can't . . ."

She didn't deserve such happiness. And supposing she spoiled it again?

"OK," he said carefully. "I can understand how you must be feeling. I'll rephrase my suggestion — let's start again. We'll pretend we're strangers who know nothing about each other, not even our names. In any case, we're probably different from what we were two years ago. I'm sure I am and, from what I've seen of you, I think you've changed more than you're hairstyle. Please, may we try?"

Poppy felt a flicker of excitement and hope. The impossible had happened: he had forgiven her. Was it also possible that they could recapture the tenderness and passion they had once shared?

"All right, Miles," she agreed. "Let's try."

She was rewarded with the smile she had thought never to see again. Then he kissed her, his lips taking hers with a feverish desperation that almost convinced her that everything would be all right.

As she returned his kiss, he murmured, "I still love you very much."

Poppy was tempted — oh, so tempted — to melt against him but, with a determination she never knew she possessed, she pushed him away. If she started kissing him now, she wouldn't be able to stop and that would never do — at least, not in a draughty car park!

"Oh no, we've never met before, remember? And I don't allow strange men to kiss me."

Miles' face fell. "I hadn't thought of

that. The quicker we get to know each other again the better. Go on, go back inside and wait for me. I'll lock the car and prepare myself for my big entrance into your life."

Poppy burst into laughter that tingled over her like newly-opened champagne. She ran lightly across the lawns and into the welcoming warmth of the clubhouse.

"What have you been doing?" Jill said as her friend sank breathlessly on to a stool at the bar. "You look as though somebody's switched on a light inside you."

"I've been outside, slaying dragons. Or, rather, green eyed monsters," Poppy said joyfully.

Miles appeared in the doorway. She fought back the illusion that the room had filled with stars and rainbows, and told herself that her main emotion should be one of caution. But it was going to be difficult. She loved him so much, and this time she must get it right.

He knew exactly where she was sitting, but he went through the motions of glancing around the room before catching sight of her. He strolled over. "Excuse me. Would you care to dance?"

Poppy rose and took his proffered hand. He led her to the dance floor. They faced each other for a moment in silence, then he said, "Hi, I'm Miles Hatherford."

Poppy searched his blue eyes for any lingering trace of mockery but his smile was warm and full of all the love in the world.

She felt that love surround her, even though he hadn't yet taken her in his arms, and returned his smile. "Hello, I'm Poppy James."

Part Two

1

"SHE really is the most remarkable child!" Jill Squires exclaimed as the baby on her lap grabbed at her necklace and shrieked with delight as her chubby fingers tangled in the bright coral beads.

Poppy Hatherford nodded enthusiastic agreement. "Of course she is. Although naming her Laura Jill and making you her godmother doesn't automatically turn her into a prodigy; Miles and I had something to do with it."

"Quite a lot," Jill agreed, holding six-month-old Laura at arm's length and admiring the luxuriant black curls and bright blue eyes. "It's no wonder she's gorgeous, with such good-looking parents. She even managed not to look like a bald old boxer when she was born."

"Jill!" her friend laughingly protested. "All babies are beautiful — to their mothers, anyway. Just wait until you have one."

161

Jill put Laura into her carrycot and regarded Poppy with a wry smile. "I'm beginning to wonder if I ever will. I've always held the old-fashioned notion that it's best if you get married first, and there's not much likelihood of that at the moment."

Poppy regarded Jill with something akin to horror. Such was her own state of wedded bliss that she advocated conversion to it with missionary zeal. "But you must! What about that Andrew somebody-or-other you brought to the christening? He seemed awfully nice."

"That was the trouble," Jill said gloomily. "He was too nice, if such a thing is possible. One of these days he'll make some woman a wonderful doormat."

Poppy giggled. "I didn't realise you liked the strong, masterful type."

"I don't, but there must be something in between. I'm not conscious of wanting any specific type, just somebody who — oh, I don't know . . . " Jill trailed lamely to a halt.

They were sitting in the small, comfortable sitting room of the flat

Jill occupied over Squires Antiques, the shop she inherited on her parents' death in a boating accident four years ago. Through the open windows streamed the high summer sun and the faint murmur of the small market town of Foxbridge going about its weekday business.

The sunlight highlighted the very different looks of the two friends. Poppy was the more obvious beauty, with her strikingly dark hair and flamboyant style. Jill, grey-eyed and ash blonde, was inclined to deprecate her own looks, not realising the attraction of her delicate bone structure and air of fragility.

Ever since Poppy, Jill's erstwhile partner and lifelong friend, had left to get married, eighteen months before, Jill had lived in the flat alone. As they sat, talking and laughing, she felt a stab of nostalgia and realised how much she missed having a really close companion; somebody in whom she could confide and share a joke. Several of her friends had moved away recently and she had to admit that she had been somewhat lonely. Despite Poppy living in London the two of them still met frequently but their priorities were no longer the same. Poppy's life now centred around Miles and Laura, and her perspective was, naturally, different from when she was single.

Jill looked around and gave an unconscious sigh. She had to admit it; at the ripe old age of twenty-seven she was turning into an old maid. The room itself bore witness to this; the half finished jigsaw puzzle spread on the table, the pile of plastic-coated library books, a bundle of knitting tucked in a corner of the armchair; all were reminders that, when the shop closed at five every evening, Jill's life closed with it.

Not that there was anything wrong with the state of spinsterhood; many women preferred and thrived on it. But Jill, although she owned a successful business, had never felt herself to be a career woman and had always assumed that she would marry and have children.

Poppy saw her friend's expression and guessed, as she always could, what she was thinking. "Why don't you try and get out more?" she said gently. "You were the one who used to nag me about sitting around getting broody. Don't you go to the country club any more?"

"Sometimes, but most of our crowd have followed your example and flown the coop, and I haven't much in common with the youngsters who go there."

"Oh dear." Poppy was getting more depressed by the minute as she visualised Jill's social life shrinking away to nothing. "Don't you see anything of that lovely man who bought the club a couple of months before I left here? He certainly livened the old place up."

"David Melbury?" Jill looked astounded. "Poppy, you know I don't get on with him!"

Poppy shrugged. "I can't think why. I thought he was rather a poppet. Not exactly handsome but very attractive in a devil-may-care sort of way. And he seemed rather keen on you until you froze him off. Still, we never did agree on our choice of men, thank goodness. Well, I don't know what to suggest. You've really got to do something to get yourself out of this terrible rut."

Jill got up and handed Poppy a letter that was sitting on the mantelpiece. "I received this last week. It's from my Aunt Harriet — you know, Mad Hattie, as she's known in the family."

"The one who lives in Brighton and breeds Siamese cats?" Poppy unfolded the letter and frowned over the four pages of careless scrawl. "Oh, I didn't realise she had a daughter. And she wants her to come and stay with you for a while. But that would be lovely!" she said, putting the letter down half read. "Just what you need to liven you up, a seventeen-year old girl around the place."

"Read on," Jill cautioned her.

Poppy read on and giggled. "She sounds a bit of a handful; ran away to London to join a rock group, wears too much make up, is cheeky and defiant — in other words, a fairly average teenager."

"But what on earth am I supposed to do with her that Aunt Hattie and Uncle Jimmy can't?" Jill asked in exasperation. "I think they'd like her to take me as some sort of role model but that's not likely, is it? She'll just see me as some old fuddy-duddy relative, a sort of maiden aunt figure who's in league with her parents to stop her enjoying herself."

"Perhaps you could take her as a role model instead," Poppy said slyly. "She seems to have a lot more fun than you do. I must admit that living in Foxbridge instead of wicked old Brighton would trim her sails a little; there's not much scope for going astray around here — as well we both know. Have you met — er — " Poppy consulted the letter again — "Prudence recently?"

"Not since she was about fourteen. She was always away at boarding school when I visited Aunt Hattie. I can scarcely remember what she looks like. Fair, like most of Mum's side of the family, and lanky, taller than me, even at that age. And she wore glasses, those wire-rimmed ones, poor kid."

As she spoke Jill conjured up a half formed mental picture of the skinny waif who had been her cousin Prudence and felt a sudden wave of sympathy. Aunt Hattie had odd ideas about most things including, probably, how to treat her teenage daughter. Perhaps poor little

Prudence was just a normal, high-spirited girl who wasn't understood by her rather elderly parents? Perhaps she needed somebody like Jill to show her some sympathy and help her do a little growing up?

"I'll do it!" she said positively. "I'll phone Aunt Hattie tonight and tell her to let Prudence come and stay here as soon as she likes. Perhaps she'd like to help me in the shop. I've never managed to find a satisfactory replacement for you."

Poppy clapped her hands and Laura joined in from her carrycot. "Good for you! I think it'll do you the world of good. I'll follow your joint progress with keen interest."

"I'm worried about Jill," Poppy said to her husband Miles over dinner that evening.

Miles chuckled "You sound like that woman who used to be on the radio."

"Mrs Dale," Poppy said absently. "No, honestly, Miles, I'm truly worried. She's vegetating in Foxbridge; she doesn't go out much; she doesn't seem to have any close friends. What can we do?"

"Jill will be all right," he tried to reassure his wife. "She's far too sensible to allow herself to turn into the recluse you're making her out to be."

"She needs taking out of herself," Poppy mused, ignoring his remark. "I asked her to close the shop for a couple of weeks and come and stay with us but she made some excuse about trade being too good at the moment. She's her own worst enemy."

"It doesn't sound like Jill, I must admit," Miles agreed. "She was always the outgoing one of the pair of you. Isn't there a man on the scene at the moment?"

"No, more's the pity. Mind you, there's not much choice in that neck of the woods. Hang on, I've had a brilliant idea."

Poppy beamed and Miles felt a surge of alarm. Poppy's brilliant ideas were well-meaning but invariably hare brained.

"It's Mohammed and the mountain all over again. If Jill won't come to London for some fun we'll have to send the fun to her. Christopher Langton, your deputy's assistant!"

Miles blinked. "Chris? What about him?"

"He was telling me, at the firm's do last week, that he's always wanted a quiet little weekend place a few miles out of London. Well, now that your mother is living with us, why don't we rent Keeper's Cottage to Chris?"

Miles' mother had lived in Foxbridge until a year ago, when Poppy and Miles had bought a large house in Hampstead complete with granny flat. It had been decided to keep her cottage as a country retreat but they had not used the place since Laura's birth.

Miles looked baffled. "Why Chris Langton?"

"Why not?" Poppy said in exasperation at his typical male stupidity. "He's very eligible; exactly what Jill needs; single, attractive, good family, bright prospects. If they get married you can arrange for him to be promoted."

"But how do you know that Jill and Chris will get on together?" he persisted, fascinated by the totally illogical workings of his otherwise practical wife's mind.

"Of course they will," Poppy scoffed.

170

"They're ideally suited. They're interested in the same things; music, the countryside, antiques — he was telling me he collects Victorian door knobs; they'll adore each other. You must speak to Chris the moment you get to the office tomorrow."

A week later, Jill, blissfully unaware of the plans being hatched on her behalf, stood in the entrance of Foxbridge Halt station awaiting the arrival of her cousin Prudence. Uncertain what image to present in her combined roles as shining example and sympathetic ally, she had brushed her thick, glossy hair out of its usual knot, and was wearing trim denim jeans and a checked shirt, all of which she hoped was a compromise between her usual buttoned-down neatness, and mutton dressed as lamb.

The ten-fifteen from Marylebone was dead on time and Jill anxiously scanned the disembarking passengers as they emerged, worried that the errant Prudence might have done a bunk somewhere between Brighton and Buckinghamshire. Only four people emerged and, as two of them were men, she was faced with the choice between greeting a young nun and a tall, spiky-haired, over-painted blonde dressed in funereal black, who looked at least as old as herself. As far as Jill knew, her cousin hadn't yet been driven to taking the veil so she approached the blonde with an outstretched hand.

"It's Prudence, isn't it? I — er — I'd have recognised you anywhere." Jill gallantly lied, hoping to make Prudence feel at home!

"Rubbish," Prudence said cheerfully. "I'll bet you were expecting some little shrimp wearing glasses and school uniform?"

"Something like that," Jill confessed. "What happened to the glasses? Contact lenses, I suppose. My, you have grown up! But don't you find all that black leather hot on a day like this?"

Prudence grinned. "You don't like it, do you? I can tell. Oh well, perhaps I am a bit overdressed for a little place like this."

That must be the understatement of the year, Jill thought as she looked around for her cousin's luggage. She hoped it wasn't the great heap of cases and bundles that the porter was wheeling towards them but, as there was nobody else there to claim it, it must be.

"For goodness sake call me Prue. And don't worry if you can't get that lot in your car," her cousin said, correctly interpreting Jill's expression. "I've got it all organised."

Just then a man came out of the station and approached them with a friendly smile; a tall, light-haired man, the sight of whom set Jill's teeth on edge. It was David Melbury. She had vaguely registered his long white estate, emblazoned with Foxbridge Country Club, sitting in the car park. He must have spent the night in London.

She was about to pretend that she hadn't seen him when Prue said, "There you are, David. I told you Jill would have a fit when she saw all my belongings. David offered to give me a lift," she explained to Jill. "We met on the train."

Jill felt a surge of alarm. She must have a talk with Prudence about the folly of speaking to strange men on trains — or anywhere else, come to that.

Shooting her young cousin an I'll-deal-with-you-later look, Jill said, "There's no need to bother Mr Melbury, Prue. I'm sure we can cope."

But David Melbury was already stowing Prue's five suitcases, two airline bags, eight carrier bags and assortment of boxed electrical appliances in his roomy vehicle. Jill was forced to admit that they would have had problems managing to pack it all in her modest Escort but she still resented being helped by him.

"It's very kind of you, David," she said in a chilly voice which she hoped belied the geniality of her statement. "We'll see you at the shop."

And taking her cousin firmly by the arm Jill steered her towards her own car.

"I get the feeling you don't like him," Prue said, as she strapped herself into the passenger seat. "Why not? He's gorgeous. I'm sure I've seen him on the telly. Tell me about him."

"What's gorgeous got to do with it?" Jill asked, turning the car around and heading for home. How could she describe David Melbury to an impressionable teenager without making him sound hopelessly glamorous?

Ten years ago he had been the golden boy of British tennis, destined to win all the honours and titles that had evaded home-grown players for so long. But a near-fatal riding accident, which had crushed one leg and put him in hospital for months, had put an end to all that. He had recovered from his injuries, but not sufficiently to play professional tennis again, and his courage and apparent lack of bitterness had won him universal admiration. For several years he remained popular and in the public eye in his role as a sports commentator on television.

All this was admirable and Jill had been as impressed as everybody else when her teenage idol moved to Foxbridge and bought the rather old-fashioned and rundown country club, but subsequent contact with him had left her conscious of vague dislike. This dislike was all the more uncomfortable because she couldn't define or rationalise it. She couldn't fault his manners or his behaviour towards her or anybody else. He was popular, hard-working and, despite ample opportunities, he wasn't a womaniser.

Jill told herself she was being churlish

whenever she stonewalled one of his friendly overtures but that didn't prevent her from doing so again the next time. Not that there had been many next times lately; Mr David Melbury appeared to have got the message that he wasn't Miss Jill Squires' cup of tea. And now he had incurred her further disapproval by ingratiating himself with her cousin, an impressionable girl at least a dozen years his junior.

'I'll soon put a stop to that,' she thought grimly as she stopped outside the antique shop. David's car pulled up behind and he jumped out, agile despite the injury that had ended his career. No wonder Prue had described him as being gorgeous, Jill observed coolly; lean and rakishly casual, with deceptively sleepy blue eyes, he was capable of turning any young girl's head without even realising he was doing it.

Jill unlocked the shop door and the three of them carried in Prue's luggage — all her worldly goods by the look of it — and dumped it on the floor amid the relics of bygone ages.

"Well, young lady," Jill said as Prue

showed signs of wanting to hang about in the shop talking to David, "upstairs with you. It's going to take you hours to unpack."

Prue pulled a face but obediently picked up two cases and headed for the staircase. David beckoned Jill over to the open door and then drew her outside. He didn't look pleased and she wondered if she had ruined any ideas he had about furthering his acquaintance with Prue.

"What's the matter with you, Jill?" His voice was quiet but angry. "You can't order Prue around like that. She's not a child."

Jill imagined how Prue must look to him, from spiky-heeled boots to spiky, bleached hair, and gave him the benefit of the doubt. She wouldn't have realised how young Prue was herself had she not known who she was.

"I know you're related but . . . " he went on.

"I'm her cousin," Jill snapped.

He feigned amazement. "You do surprise me. From the way you're carrying on I thought you were at least her granny. She's . . . "

177

"Seventeen," Jill cut in again. "She's seventeen, David."

This time his amazement was genuine. "I'm sorry, I didn't realise. I thought she was at least as old as you."

"Me and Methuselah, I suppose?" Jill said drily.

David tried to look hurt. "You know that's not what I meant. Tell me, Jill, why do you dislike me so much?"

His frankness shook her and she felt a discomforting blush warm her cheeks. To deny her dislike of him would be dishonest; to confirm it would mean justifying it, to him and to herself, and that was impossible because there was no definite reason.

He was watching her intently, his blue eyes sleepy no longer, but sharp and inquisitive. His long lashes were tipped with gold, and his thick, light brown hair had taken on the colour of the sun. Jill found herself thinking that he must have been very blond when he was a small boy.

Help, this would never do! Lifting her determined chin in the air, she said, "You must excuse me, I have to go and organise Prue."

He knew that his question was impossible to answer and his soft, mocking laugh seemed to follow her through the shop and up into the flat. Prue had transferred her mountain of luggage upstairs and into what she had correctly guessed to be her bedroom. It was Poppy's old room and the individual decor — Thirties film posters tacked over rag-rolled walls — met with Prue's approval.

"It's smashing," she enthused as Jill joined her. "But I think I might need another wardrobe."

'At least!' Jill thought as Prue began to unpack, flinging armfuls of clothing on to the bed and over chairs until the room resembled a boutique in the grip of the January sales. Who on earth had paid for them all? Aunt Hattie had spent a fortune on Prue's education but she wasn't the sort to subsidise her daughter's more frivolous expenditures.

One large cardboard box was packed with records and tapes, the covers of which were illustrated with pictures of the bizarre looking creatures upon whom Prue obviously modelled herself. Jill pulled a secret face and resigned herself to having her peace — and her ears — shattered, although the sight of Prue's Walkman was some comfort.

"Why don't you leave that and come and have a cup of tea or coffee?" she invited the young girl. "I'll give you a hand to settle in later. I've closed the shop for the day in your honour so there's no rush."

In the small, sunny kitchen they faced each other across the table, each conscious of the other's scrutiny. Jill could see that, behind the warpaint, Prue had grown into an extremely pretty girl, and was gratified to note a definite family likeness between them; the same even features and unusual grey eyes. And if Prue's eyebrows were anything to go by, her hair had been the same dark ash blonde as Jill's before it was bleached and cut to within an inch of it's life.

She met Jill's gaze with a cheeky grin. "Well, cousin Jill, what has Mother been telling you about me; that I'm the black sheep of the family?"

"No," Jill said truthfully; Aunt Hattie

180

hadn't used that term exactly although the implication had been there. "She just said — well, I got the impression that you and she don't see eye to eye over certain things and she thought that for you to come and stay with me for a while might — er . . . "

Golly, it was hard work and Prue's wry smile wasn't helping. Jill had taken an instant liking to her cousin and sympathised with her plight. Being packed off to stay in a deadly dull place with a 'respectable' relative, like a heroine in a Victorian novel, was a pretty dire fate for a lively teenager. And being such was Prue's only crime, Jill was sure.

"Well, anyway, I'll do my best to make you comfortable and — er — entertain you," she concluded.

Prue looked disappointed. "Mother didn't mention my running away from school and then away from home? And my unsuitable friends, and . . . "

Jill didn't want to hear any more in case she began to regret having invited this self-confessed delinquent into her home. Anyway, she was sure that Prue was exaggerating; making her behaviour sound far worse than it had been, simply as a means of drawing attention to herself.

"We all make mistakes," she said lightly. "Looking back, I'm sure I drove my parents to distraction when I was your age. Now, have you thought about getting a job? If you've nothing special in mind I'll pay you the going rate to help me out in the shop."

Prue's face lit up. "Would you? How super! I was dreading looking for work. There can't be many jobs going in a small, out of the way place like this, especially for somebody of my limited talents."

"Why do you say that? You're intelligent and educated up to the eyebrows. What did you train to be at that posh school you went to?"

Prue looked rather shamefaced. "Nothing very worthwhile. I could never decide what I wanted to be and kept switching courses. I've had several jobs since I left school at Christmas, in shops mostly, so I'll feel at home working for you. My last one was in a boutique." She giggled. "I

182

spent all my wages buying the clothes at discount prices."

Jill smiled sympathetically, recalling her own clothes-mad youth. "There's not much danger of you being to tempted to buy the stock here. Well, Prue, have a couple of days to settle in and start work on Monday."

"Great. In the meantime I'll look the town over, see what there is on offer in the way of entertainment."

Jill gave a faint sigh as she imagined her cousin's disappointment at how little there was to do in Foxbridge. Prue appeared to be sophisticated beyond her years, even by today's standards, and Jill feared that within a short time she was going to have a very bored young lady on her hands.

2

"**P**RUE'S a dear," Jill assured Poppy when they spoke on the phone a week later. "Honestly, I don't know why Aunt Hattie was fussing about her. She's just a normal, high-spirited seventeen-year-old. Her taste in music leaves a lot to be desired and she seems to be against reading books on principle — I think it smacks too much of school, where I don't think she was terribly happy — but it's not up to me to criticise her taste. She looks a bit out of place among all the antiques but the customers seem to like her, especially the tourists."

Poppy snorted with laughter. "A fine example of genuine British punk, in mint condition; had any offers for her yet?"

Jill scowled to herself. "I had to warn David Melbury off. Although, to be fair to him, she does look much older than she is when she's all dressed up. When are you going to come down and meet her for yourself? You and the family haven't used the cottage for ages."

"No, and we won't, not this year anyway. We've leased it to one of Miles' chums at work for the rest of the summer; he'll be using it at weekends. Aren't you pleased?"

"Why should I be?" Jill asked suspiciously. "Unless he's paying the rent into my bank account."

"He's single and very dishy," Poppy explained patiently. "I've told him all about you and he's going to pop into the shop as soon as he arrives. Honestly, Jill, you'll like him."

"Don't bet on it!" Jill threatened, hanging up after adding a brief farewell. Honestly! What was Poppy thinking of?

"You look a teeny bit miffed about something," Prue observed, returning from fetching their elevenses from the nearby patisserie. "They'd sold out of apple Danish so I got you a Chelsea bun instead, all right?"

Jill nodded absently. "Fine. Tell me, Prue, what would you do if your best friend told you that she'd arranged for some sort of permanent blind date to come and live on your doorstep?"

"Put the flags out," Prue said practically. "It's not the sort of opportunity you get very often in a one horse town like this. If you don't want him I'll have him — since you did such a good job of warning David Melbury off. He practically runs the other way when he sees me coming."

"Good!" Jill said grimly. "He's totally unsuitable. He's a lot older than you and he has, as they say, been around."

A description guaranteed to make him appear even more alluring to her cousin, she realised as soon as the words had left her mouth, but Prue merely grinned. "Yes, Mum."

Jill's good humour returned. "Don't be cheeky, young Prudence," she said, laughing. "Eight and a half years does not constitute a generation gap. At least, I hope it doesn't."

"Of course not, but why don't ·you prove it by coming to the country club with me tonight. Melanie, the girl who works in the patisserie, was just telling me there's a disco there on Fridays and Saturdays."

Jill screwed up her face. Crowded discos were her idea of hell on earth but Prue was looking at her with such ingenuous delight that Jill couldn't refuse. "Oh, all right, but only if I can sit out in the bar, well away from the noise."

"You're a good sport, Jill. You should get out more, you know. I'll lend you something to wear, if you like."

Prue's suggestion wasn't as ludicrous as it sounded. Not all of her outfits were totally bizarre and she coaxed Jill into a silky, leopard print top and pants which she wouldn't have dreamed of buying for herself, but which she had to admit looked good on her.

"That's great," Prue enthused, coming into Jill's bedroom to inspect the result. She was wearing a purple suede minidress and had painted everything — lids, lips, cheeks and nails — to match. The result was unnerving to say the least! "Now sit down and I'll do your hair."

Jill sat and apprehensively allowed Prue to attack her heavy glossy hair with a selection of heated tongs, styling rods and spiky brushes. She was going to refuse politely but firmly if Prue offered

187

to do her face as well!

"You won't damage it with all those implements, will you?" she asked nervously.

"No, I'll be very careful. You've got super hair," the younger girl enthused. "Mine was the same lovely, streaky ash blonde before I started messing about with it."

"Why did you do it?" Jill asked in astonishment.

Prue gave a shamefaced grin. "To annoy Mother, I suppose. That's why I did most of the things I did."

"Prue!" Jill scolded. "That wasn't nice. Imagine how bad you'd feel if you suddenly lost your parents, like I did."

Prue nodded, refusing to meet Jill's eyes in the mirror. "I know. Tell you what; do you think she'd be pleased if I grew my hair back to normal?"

"I'm sure she would," Jill said gently. "It wouldn't be such a trial for you, would it?"

Prue shook her spiky blonde head. "Not really. It's a real pain, having it trimmed and the roots retouched every couple of weeks. I'll have a sort through my clothes, as well, and throw out some of the more outrageous stuff. You were right; that black leather is horrendously hot this weather. I think I'll cultivate a new image to go with my surroundings. I can just see myself in jodhpurs and shiny brown riding boots."

"Don't throw your old clothes away," Jill said practically. "I'll give anything you don't want to the vicar's wife."

Prue stared. "Will they suit her?"

Jill laughed until her mascara ran at the idea of plump, sensible Mrs Protheroe striding around the parish in a fringed leather miniskirt and sequinned vest.

"No, they wouldn't, not at all," she finally gasped, "but she'll be glad of them to sell for charity at the August bank holiday fete next month."

Prue swept the loose waves and curls she had created to one side of Jill's head and anchored them with a big, gold butterfly clip. "There. What do you think?"

"Not bad," Jill admitted. "Not bad at all."

"You'll knock 'em dead tonight," Prue

predicted, and Jill resisted the impulse to reply, "Who?"

At seventeen life was all breathless anticipation and uncertainty. Who was Jill to cast a cynical light on the evening ahead?

David Melbury had done a good job of revitalising Foxbridge country club, Jill had to admit. The Victorian building had been beautifully restored, and the additional facilities — indoor pool and tennis courts, a gym and a vegetarian restaurant — were housed in low, modern buildings which were hidden from general view by a dense screen of shrubs. The original building was now devoted to entertainment, with several bars and clubrooms catering for the members' different tastes.

The disco was being held in what had been the old ballroom, now fitted out with a sound system and laser lights which would have astounded the original occupants of the house. After signing Prue in and making arrangements for her to become a member, Jill sought out the Regency bar, which she knew from previous experience was the one farthest away from the racket of the disco.

There was only a handful of other people in the bar and, as Jill didn't know any of them well enough to join them, she took refuge at a table half concealed behind a large potted palm. Solitary drinking, either in public or in private, had never been to her taste and she began to wish that she hadn't come. But Prue had been so thrilled at the prospect, and Jill found herself smiling as she reflected that an event which her cousin would have considered run-of-the-mill in Brighton, had taken on great allure in sleepy Foxbridge.

"Hallo, Jill, you're an unexpected visitor. What are you doing among the greenery? Are you hiding or have you a secret assignation with somebody?"

It was David Melbury, looking irritatingly attractive in a dark grey formal suit.

As he dropped into the chair opposite her, she decided to have another try at getting along with him. "I confess it; I'm hiding. I came with Prue to the disco but it's not really my thing, so I've taken refuge in here."

He raised a sarcastic eyebrow. "I know she's young but surely she doesn't need a chaperon?"

"She asked me to come — and as she's not yet a member, she couldn't have got her in on her own," Jill pointed out, her feeling of benevolence towards him slipping rapidly away.

David smiled. "I stand corrected." He lounged back in the chair, his long lean body graceful and relaxed. His deceptively sleepy gaze was searching, and Jill resisted the urge to fiddle with her new hair-do. He was probably thinking how peculiar she was, dressed up to the nines and lurking in a dark corner.

But he said, "I like your hair like that," and immediately looked cross with himself, as though the casual remark had slipped out unbidden.

'Don't fret, David,' Jill thought cynically. One careless compliment won't have me joining the hordes of women who chase shamelessly after you.

There was a long uncomfortable silence which David filled by asking Jill if she'd like another glass of wine. She refused as graciously as she could and he rose to leave. When he finally vanished Jill found that she had been holding her breath, and she let it out in a long relieved sigh. He affected her in much the same way as an off-key note of music, ruffling her calm and setting her teeth on edge.

She realised that she would like another drink and, making sure that David was out of sight — after all, she had no reason to offend him — she emerged from her corner and walked over to the bar. The room had filled up during the evening, and Jill found herself standing next to a well-dressed stranger who was also waiting to be served.

"After you." He stood aside and let her give the barman her order; then he used this as an excuse to say, "It's nice here, isn't it? Do you come here often?"

Jill stared at him open-mouthed, partly because she had never actually heard anybody utter this banal phrase outside of a comedy routine, but mostly because of the man who had said it. In his late twenties, tall and dark, with a profile which would have had Lord Byron sobbing with envy, he had to be the handsomest man Jill had ever set eyes on. She presumed that with his physical advantages he didn't have to worry too much about his chat-up lines being madly original!

She cast desperately around for a suitable riposte but he was ahead of her. "Won't you join me? I've just arrived here and I don't know a soul."

Only the previous evening Jill had been lecturing Prue on the evils of speaking to strange men, but she conveniently forgot this as she took in the melting brown eyes fringed with lashes most models would kill for. "Thank you," she murmured.

When they had been served she led him to the table she had been occupying all evening, grateful for its seclusion. It would be terrible if she was trampled in the rush when the other women in the room caught sight of him.

"You're new to Foxbridge?" she asked him, admiring the way his thick hair curled around his well-shaped ears.

"Arrived today," he replied. "I'm only here for the weekend but it's the first of many, I hope."

He managed to imply that he had been in doubt about the wisdom of staying, but now that he had met Jill, it would take wild horses to drive him away. It was heady stuff and Jill took a hasty sip of wine to clear her throat.

"Are you staying with friends or at a hotel?"

He smiled, revealing white, even teeth and a fetching dimple in one lean cheek. "I'm renting a weekend cottage here. I've always wanted a little place in the country, and when a friend at work offered me his on very reasonable terms, I jumped at the chance."

'Good heavens above!' Jill thought faintly. 'He must be Miles' friend from the office, and he's staying at Keeper's Cottage. Oh, thank you, Poppy, thank you!'

Then she came down to earth with a bump as the stranger went on, "The only problem is I'm under something of an obligation to be nice to a friend of my friend's wife; some boring old spinster who runs a shop in town."

"Did they actually tell you she was a boring old spinster?" Jill asked in an ominously calm voice.

He laughed. "Well no, they wouldn't,

195

would they? But I can read between the lines. If she's as interesting and attractive as I've been told, my friends wouldn't have been so insistent about my looking her up."

"That's rather cynical, isn't it? Perhaps they simply think the two of you will get on well together?" Jill said, hoping that he would agree with her. She wanted so much for him not to be as shallow as he appeared.

To her relief he said, "Perhaps you're right. I might get a pleasant surprise when I pop into her shop tomorrow morning and make myself known."

More like a nasty shock! Jill wondered which would be the least embarrassing, to introduce herself to him now or wait until the unsuspecting stranger walked into the shop tomorrow? She would wait, she decided; it would give her time to collect her thoughts and decide what sort of attitude to take.

She stood up and picked up her bag. "I must go, I want to see how my young cousin is enjoying herself in the disco."

The stranger also rose. "I hope we'll meet again."

Jill gave him an enigmatic smile. "Oh, I've no doubts about that. It's such a small town we couldn't help it if we tried."

★ ★ ★

"So you enjoyed yourself last night?" Jill asked Prue as they meandered about the shop early next morning, flicking dusters over the stock.

Prue nodded her bright head, adorned this morning with a red and white spotted bandeau tied in a large bow, like a cartoon Easter egg. "It was fun. I've been invited to two parties and a barbecue. If it goes on like this I might never go home. Do you think you could stand that?" she joked.

Jill considered the question seriously. "I could stand it very easily."

Prue was proving to be good company, with little or no sign of the problems about which Aunt Hattie had dropped such dark hints. She was industrious and eager to please. Whether this would wear off along with the novelty of living in different surroundings remained to be seen, but Jill was unstinting in her praise when she sent a brief progress report to Aunt Hattie.

And, after all, if Prue hadn't whisked her off to the country club last night, Jill wouldn't have met whatever-his-name-was; Miles and Poppy's friend. She knew she would see him again this morning but she was grateful that she was now forearmed with the comforting knowledge that he had spoken to her for her own sake, and had not approached her under duress as a 'boring old spinster' into whose life he had been ordered to bring a little sunshine.

They were busier than usual that morning. Foxbridge was a pretty little town set in the rolling Chilterns, and a convenient stopping off point for the coachloads of trippers meandering about that stretch of countryside. There were three other antique shops close to Squires but they all did satisfactory business as the tourists rushed to buy up bits and pieces of Merrie Olde England to take home with them.

Jill was tidying herself to go to lunch when Prue lounged into the small cloakroom-cum-office at the back of the shop. "There's a chap out front who wants to speak to you personally."

In the rush Jill had almost forgotten about the visitor she was expecting. "What's he like?" she asked Prue, curious as to her opinion of him, and wondering how the girl could be so casual in the face of such outrageous good looks.

Prue frowned as though she had trouble recalling the man to whom she had just spoken. "Just a chap. Dark, youngish — a bit too pleased with himself for my taste."

Jill smiled wryly to herself as she went into the shop; one woman's meat was evidently another's poison. But Prue's indifference to him was apparently exceptional. Even as Jill felt a shock of purely aesthetic pleasure at the sight of his patrician profile etched against the window, she noticed the reaction of the lady customers in the shop. The three American matrons were ogling him with much the same mixture of awe and delight with which they had earlier been examining an exquisite Wedgewood vase.

Jill hesitated for a moment, unsure of her ground. Then she relaxed, amused by her uncertainty; it wasn't worth worrying about. If anyone was entitled to be offended by the situation it was she rather than the stranger.

She went up to him as he stood leafing through some old magazines, and said quietly, "Hallo, I'm Jill Squires."

He swung around and his expression changed almost comically from surprise to pleasure. "Well, well, aren't you the sly one? I suppose I deserve a shock like this for calling you rude names. I'm Chris Langton."

They shook hands and Jill began to apologise for any embarrassment she might have caused him, but he made a sweeping gesture of dismissal. "Don't worry, please. It serves me right for my habit of telling my troubles to ladies in bars — but I'm afraid I shall go on doing it; I enjoy it too much to stop."

Jill stared at him for a long astonished moment and then began to laugh, an attractive, merry sound which had everybody else in the shop smiling even though they didn't know the joke. She decided at that moment that she liked Chris Langton, and that having him around was going to be fun. He was vain, self-centered and a male chauvinist of the worse possible kind but he was so painfully honest about it that it was impossible to be angry with him. And she had the additional relief of knowing that, beautiful as he was, there was no way he was going to touch her heart. Any woman who fell for Chris — and their numbers were surely legion — would always play second fiddle to his ego.

"Nice place you have here," he said, looking around. "Do you have any Victorian door knobs? I collect them."

Jill wondered if he was pulling her leg but his brown eyes were perfectly serious. It was a relief to discover that he was interested in something else besides himself. "No, I'm afraid not. We're at the height of the tourist season and all the smaller stuff gets snapped up as soon as it comes in. If I come across any in my travels I'll keep them for you."

"Would you? I'd be awfully grateful. Mind you, I think the best place to find them is in skips outside old houses which are being pulled down or converted."

The picture of Chris, immaculate this morning in pale grey slacks and a lavender pullover, ferreting around rubbish skips, was an intriguing one and Jill wondered if there might be more to him than met the eye.

"I was hoping you would have lunch with me," he went on.

Jill laughed without rancour. "No, you weren't. You thought I was going to be a boring old spinster."

He had the grace to look ashamed. "Ouch, you don't pull your punches, do you? I'm sorry about that; I'd had rather a trying day at work. Well, obviously I thought you were worth speaking to last night, so you know my motives in asking you out today are sincere."

Or as sincere as a man like Chris's motives can be, Jill reflected as she fetched her bag from the office.

"Are you going out with him?" Prue hissed, following her to the back of the shop. "I know his type. He's a poser."

Jill smiled serenely. "I know. But I've a feeling that being seen around with a gorgeous creature like Chris will be like wearing mink and diamonds; it won't be the most intellectually or emotionally satisfying experience in the world, but it will do wonders for my ego — and it could be a lot of fun."

Prue gave a disapproving sniff. "I suppose it's all right so long as you realise that's all it is and don't go imagining yourself in love with him."

★ ★ ★

Chris Langton was, as Jill had predicted to herself and to her dubious cousin, a highly entertaining companion. As well as lunch, he took her out to dinner the same evening at The Gourmet's Kitchen, the best restaurant in town. He was an ideal date providing you weren't looking for deep commitment or passionate avowals of love. He was elegant, good-natured and had an outrageous line in gossipy conversation which was funny without being spiteful.

He was, in short, everything Jill needed to brighten up her life, without the complication of wondering whether or not he was going to break her heart, and she told Poppy so on the phone the following morning.

"But that's not what I planned at all!" Poppy exclaimed in dismay. "You and Chris were supposed to take one look at each other and fall madly in love."

"I think he does that every morning when he shaves," Jill said drily. "I'm sorry, Poppy, I haven't the slightest intention of falling for him. For one thing, I couldn't stand the strain of spending the rest of my life wondering if he'd been snaffled up by another woman while my back was turned; you must admit he's rather irresistible."

"But not to you," Poppy said rather huffily, disappointed that her manoeuvring hadn't worked in quite the way she had hoped. "Oh well, at least he's managed to prise you out of that flat. It's a pity he'll only be in Foxbridge at weekends. I'll have to leave it up to Prue to organise your social life during the rest of the week."

"I do not need organising!" Jill said crossly. "And please don't bother to send any more young men for me to fall in love with! I was quite happy with my life the way it was before you and Prudence interfered."

But when she'd hung up Jill reflected that she wasn't being quite honest with Poppy or herself. She had enjoyed herself over the past couple of days and the future looked a lot brighter than it had done a few weeks ago before Poppy and Prue had begun to 'organise' her. For the first time in ages she began to look forward and wonder what the future held in store.

3

THE fortnightly meeting of the All Saints charity committee had been going on for hours, or so it seemed to Jill as she sat listening to her six fellow members each pressing to have her own pet idea for the autumn fete adopted.

"Do you really think fortune telling is quite — er, well, quite nice at a church fete?" asked Miss Tidy who ran the old fashioned draper's shop in town, and who was against any form of innovation. "I mean, dabbling in the occult and that sort of thing."

"But it won't be real fortune telling," Mrs Protheroe, the vicar's wife, protested impatiently. It was her idea and she was defending it for all she was worth. "It will just be one of us pretending to be a gypsy or a soothsayer or whatever. People love that sort of thing; it will be a real money-spinner and that's what this is all about, isn't it?"

She beamed encouragingly at her companions and there were murmurs of agreement. This year the money they raised was going towards building an indoor swimming pool at the local junior school.

"It won't be difficult," she went on. "Nearly all the customers will be people we know; it will just be a matter of telling them what you think they would like to hear. It's a perfectly harmless bit of fun. Jill, perhaps you'd care to have a shot at it?"

Jill wrenched her attention away from contemplation of the vicar's wonderful garden and tried to recall what was being discussed. "Er — I'm running the bric-a-brac stall, as usual. I'm supposed to be able to spot the more valuable stuff and make sure that it isn't sold for pennies rather than pounds."

"Haven't you got an assistant who could do that while you tell fortunes?" the chairman, Mrs Biggs-Wallace, asked.

The subject of the discussion was filtering into Jill's consciousness and she had an alarming picture of herself, draped in clanking jewellery and veils, shut away in a dark, hot tent instead of enjoying the sunshine which always blessed the church fete. She devoted a fair chunk of her time to the committee's fund-raising activities; this time she was going to put her foot down; somebody else could play at being fortune teller.

"It's impossible. Prue's only been learning the trade for a couple of weeks; she's far too inexperienced. We don't want another Van Rieman affair."

There was a solemn hush around the table as they recalled the catastrophe of two years ago. Jill had had tonsillitis and her stall had been assigned to a person who didn't know the difference between jumble and genuine treasure. A dingy, unframed painting of a grim-faced woman had been sold for two pounds to a sharp-eyed dealer. It had turned out to be a long-lost Dutch masterpiece and was subsequently sold at auction for thousands of pounds.

"Quite right, my dear," Mrs Biggs-Wallace agreed. "That was a catastrophe. When I think of the worthwhile things we could have done with all that money. I suppose your young assistant wouldn't care to try her hand at fortune telling?"

"Oh no," Jill said hastily; Prue wouldn't thank her for volunteering her for such a thankless task. "She — um, I believe she suffers from claustrophobia. Anyway, I've put her down for the second-hand clothes stall."

"If Mrs Protheroe ever sympathises with you about your claustrophobia, don't deny having it," Jill said upon her return to the shop.

Prue looked up in amazement from the horse brasses she was polishing. "Why?"

Jill flopped into a chair, enervated by the meeting and the heatwave which was gripping their part of the country, and closed her eyes. "Don't ask; it's too complicated to explain. Any customers while I was away?"

"Three." Prue enumerated the sales and added in a too casual voice, "Oh yes, David Melbury dropped in."

"Oh?" Jill was instantly the suspicious mother hen. "What did he want?"

Prue pulled a regretful face. "Not me, more's the pity. He was with a woman; attractive but stuck-up, all pearls and heavy perfume. She carried on as though she owned the place."

Jill recognised the description immediately. "Sally Crawshaw. As it happens she does own the place. Her husband held quite a few of the leases on the property around here and Sally inherited the lot — leases, big house, tenant farms and all — when he died a couple of years ago."

"Died? Golly, she doesn't look old enough to be widow."

"She's twenty-seven, like me; we went to school together," Jill said. "Charley must have been twice her age at least. He adored her; spoiled her rotten."

"It shows," Prue agreed. "She was after that set of mother-of pearl combs we had in the window last week — threw a right tantrum when I said they'd been sold. David looked most uncomfortable. Is she his regular girl friend?"

"Depends which one of them you ask; she'll say yes, he'll say no. I don't think he's the type to settle down with one woman."

"Pity," Prue murmured and Jill experienced a moment's disquiet. Until now Prue had been a model of good behaviour, but only possibly because everything had so far gone her way. If she was nursing a bad crush on David Melbury who knows what she might do to attract his attention.

To incur Sally's displeasure was not pleasant, as Jill knew from personal experience. It didn't take much to upset Sally; Jill's only crime had been to argue mildly about a couple of petty clauses in her lease; anyone trying to snaffle Sally's latest man would rouse her to anger of earthshaking proportions.

Jill had always felt rather ambivalent about Sally. They had known each other since childhood and, apart from the business with the lease, which had soon blown over, they usually got on well together. But only, Jill admitted to herself, because she worked at it; she hated rows, and it suited her not to fall out with her landlady. So when Sally returned alone to the shop the next day Jill found herself trying to soften the blow Sally had suffered in not getting exactly what she wanted.

"The combs wouldn't have suited you, Sally. To be absolutely honest — " Jill looked around the shop and lowered her voice — "they were a bit cheap and nasty. I'd have advised you against buying them."

Sally pouted. "But they were so pretty. I've bought this red, Spanish-looking number to wear at my summer ball next week. I thought, if I put my hair up, like this . . . "

As Sally waffled on, preening and demonstrating how she planned to wear her long, dark hair, Jill fought hard to stop her eyes glazing over. How on earth did an intelligent man like David Melbury put up with this silly, self-centered creature?

"You did get your invitation, didn't you?" Sally went on. "Of course, it's a frantic bore, all the preparation, but everybody expects it."

The summer ball at the magnificent Georgian residence of the Crawshaw family was an event which had been going on for generations, but Jill suspected that Sally was less interested in tradition than on seizing an annual opportunity to queen it over the locals.

"Who will you be coming with?" Sally chattered on. "I hope you've got a decent partner. Heaven knows there isn't much of a selection around here. David will be my official escort, of course."

Her tone implied that she would be the only one there with a man fit to be seen in public with, and Jill smiled to herself. Chris Langton had agreed to accompany her; his stunning good looks, enhanced by evening dress, would wipe that self-satisfied look off Sally's face.

"Just some boring chum of Poppy's," she murmured, deciding to keep Chris under wraps until next weekend.

As Sally left the shop she passed a man on his way in. He watched her progress up the High Street for several seconds before turning to Jill and saying, "That was Mrs Crawshaw, wasn't it?"

Jill nodded. "That's right."

"Thought so. I don't know her to speak to but I was a friend of her late husband."

He was about Charley's age, Jill reckoned; a fresh-faced, upright man with a spectacular head of prematurely white hair. There was something vaguely military about him and Jill said, "Were you in the army with Mr Crawshaw?"

He nodded. "Bosom chums, me and Charley but we lost touch. Always meant to look him up but never got around to it. Lovely old house he had. Still in the family, I suppose?"

"Yes. Mrs Crawshaw still lives there," Jill confirmed.

"Fancy. You'd think she would have remarried, an attractive woman like that."

Jill raised her eyebrows at such a personal remark but she replied evenly, "No, she hasn't remarried. What may I do for you? Did you want something in particular or are you just browsing?"

The man smiled, not at all put out by her sudden formality. "Just browsing. I know nothing about antiques but I like the look of some of these old things. Now, Charley had a superb collection of paintings and furniture."

But Jill refused to be drawn any further on the subject of the Crawshaws and the man left without buying anything.

That evening, as Jill took her turn at preparing the supper, an excited shriek summoned her into the living room where Prue was watching a documentary programme about Wimbledon Lawn Tennis Club.

"Look, it's David, when he nearly won the title. Isn't he gorgeous?" Prue babbled.

"I remember this game," Jill murmured, perching on the edge of a chair and resting her chin on her hand. "I think every girl in my form played truant to stay home and watch it."

She had been seventeen the year David Melbury reached the semi-finals of the men's singles. He had lost, but not without taking the pugnacious American champion to five hard-fought sets. Experience won in the end and David was gracious but optimistic in defeat. Next year he would win, he predicted in the interview afterwards, happily unaware that it was his last game. Three weeks later, on an early morning ride through the peaceful lanes of Hampshire, his mount, startled by a noisy motor bike, had bolted, slipped and fallen on David, crushing his leg.

Along with the rest of his fans, Jill had been shattered by the news, and as she sat there, ten years later, watching his lithe, beautifully co-ordinated figure bounding about the court, she felt a return of the sadness. How had he borne the disappointment? He never appeared bitter but how must he feel when he saw a reprise of his marvellous, lost talent? Maybe it had affected him more deeply than he cared to show.

Jill sighed and returned to the kitchen. No matter how she pitied David Melbury, she feared that she would never shake off the tiny niggle of dislike she felt whenever she met him.

With the coming of August, the usual showery, changeable summer had turned tropical, and southern England basked beneath seemingly endless, cloudless blue skies. By the third week the novelty had worn off and the ungrateful population was bemoaning the lack of rain and predicting a hard winter, as though everything, even Mother Nature's benevolence, had a price.

Much as Jill revelled in the heat, she had to admit, as she put the final touches to her appearance for the Crawshaw summer ball, that she would have preferred to go for a cooling drive in the country. Fortunately, her choice of a simple, white cotton broderie anglaise evening dress looked and felt cool. She avoided both heavy make-up and jewellery, and swept the thickness of her hair up off her neck into a knot of loose waves on top of her head.

"Shouldn't you wear a bit more make-up with all that ghostly white?" Prue asked critically as she lolled on Jill's bed, watching the proceedings.

"I don't think so." Jill surveyed herself anxiously in the long mirror and teased a few tendrils of hair around her ears and neck. "I don't need it with this tan, and it'll only smudge in the heat. Whew! Quite honestly I could do without going tonight. I can think of a lot of other things I'd rather be doing."

"I can't," Prue said. "I'm really fed up, being left at home on a Saturday night like Cinderella."

"You'd hate it," Jill said honestly. "It's not your thing at all. I can't think why you've made up your mind you're missing out on something."

But she could guess. Prue had taken no interest in tonight's party until it

217

occurred to her that David Melbury would be there, and since then she had alternately sulked and played the neglected waif in the hope that Jill would take pity on her and ask Sally to issue another invitation. But Jill had, with great difficulty, hardened her heart, and refused to submit to such emotional blackmail.

"Weren't you and Melanie going to the cinema tonight?" Jill asked patiently.

Prue wrinkled her nose. "It's far too hot to be shut up indoors."

"Then you certainly wouldn't want to be stuck in a stuffy old ballroom all evening," Jill said briskly.

"But they were putting up a marquee when I went past there today, and fairy lights in the trees," Prue wailed. "It'll be beautiful with the gardens all lit up; so romantic."

Jill's tender heart melted. Oh, the agony of being seventeen and imagining yourself in love! Whether by accident or design, Prue was managing to look especially pathetic tonight. Her bleached crop of hair was growing out in lank, untidy streaks, and her skimpy shorts and tee shirt made her look all arms and legs.

Jill went over and sat on the bed, putting her arm around the desolate teenager's shoulders. "I know what this is all about, love, and I do sympathise. But you hardly know him. And he's completely wrong for you . . . "

Prue jerked fiercely away from Jill. "Kindly let me be the judge of that! How could you possibly know what's right or wrong for me? You sound just like Mother."

'Oops!' Jill thought. The generation gap she had thought didn't exist was suddenly yawning between them like the Grand Canyon; drastic action was called for. Taking her car keys from the dressing table, she dropped them into Prue's lap.

"Here, why don't you and Melanie go to that dance in Aylesbury you saw advertised? I know you're not old enough to drive but Melanie has a licence. You won't have to worry about missing the last train if you have your own transport. But be sure you tell her, no drinking and driving!"

Prue cheered up a little. Her requests

that she and Melanie borrow the car were usually refused. "Of course not. Thanks, Jill, that's sweet of you."

The bell rang and Jill picked up her bag. "Here's Chris. Now, mind how you go tonight. I've only got one car — and one cousin." Prue smiled and Jill felt on safe enough ground to add jokingly, "I am sorry, Cinders, but I'm afraid this is one night when you can't go to the ball."

Chris looked gratifyingly spectacular in a white tuxedo. And his approving whistle when he saw Jill was equally gratifying. To have captured the attention of a man like Chris was flattering to say the least, and Jill wondered if she deserved it. Not because she wasn't worthy but because she didn't extend her appreciation beyond the occasional goodnight peck on the cheek. But he never pressed her to do so and she assumed that he had a more serious female commitment in town. He never mentioned it and she discreetly didn't ask. On their four or five dates they had become friends, nothing more; Chris's love-life was his own business.

The Crawshaw residence was decked

out in spectacular fashion with floodlighting in the trees showing the lovely house and grounds to their best advantage. The guests had already started to overflow from the ballroom and the scene was, as Prue had predicted, a romantic one, as the formally dressed couples drifted over the long lawns. The rose-covered walks and arbours were interspersed with rustic furniture, and an artificial waterfall trickled over rockeries and past statuary into a broad, bright stream.

Jill and Chris entered through the open front door to be greeted by their hostess, striking in the red dress she had described to Jill. Sally's good breeding prevented her jaw from dropping open on being introduced to Jill's escort but it didn't stop her saying, "My word, sweetie, you're a dark horse. Where did you find him?"

"He wandered into the shop one day," Jill said truthfully.

"Well, be sure and let me know when you're finished with him," Sally replied, looking up at Chris from beneath her lashes.

He grinned, not one whit abashed at

being discussed as if he wasn't there. "Easy, girls, I'm only here at weekends."

"Pity," Sally murmured, bustling away to greet further new arrivals, and leaving Jill reflecting that their hostess's attachment to David Melbury couldn't be that strong if she could flirt so shamelessly with another man.

"You don't want to dance, do you?" Chris pleaded, looking at the handful of couples drifting desultorily about the dance floor. "It's far too warm. Let's take some champagne down by the water. I'll tell you how lovely you look in the moonlight and swear my undying love."

"Oh, please don't!" Jill said, alarmed that he might be serious. "Let's go and mingle with the other guests instead."

Chris snorted with laughter. "Safety in numbers, eh? I've been developing a healthy sense of humility ever since I met you, Jill. You aren't simply playing hard to get, are you?"

"No, I am not!" she said definitely, taking him by the hand and towing him towards the long, open windows. "Come on, let's see if we can find somebody who appreciates your charms more than I do — apart from Sally; she's spoken for."

The evening wore on and the pace slowed even more as the warm night and cold champagne took their toll. The small orchestra played to an almost empty ballroom as everybody took to the gardens. The rustic furniture accommodated only a few guests and the others settled on the grass, the women's dresses looking like huge exotic flowers.

Towards midnight Jill found herself wandering down towards the stream, and she glanced briefly over her shoulder to ascertain that Chris wasn't following her to carry out his threat. The evening had been too pleasant to spoil it with glib, insincere protestations of love, no matter how light-hearted and well intentioned they were.

She leaned against the sloping trunk of a willow, a slender wraith in her white gown, and watched the tree's delicate fronds trailing in the sluggish current of clear water. She had enjoyed the evening far more than she had expected to, renewing acquaintances she had neglected and finding her old friends more forgiving than she deserved.

Only the chuckle of the water and the faint strains of distant music broke the stillness, so footfalls in the dry remains of last year's leaves sounded louder than they usually would have done. Jill stood still and silent, hoping to remain undetected by whoever it was, but a familiar voice said, "I'm always finding you hiding behind trees lately."

Resisting an urge to click her tongue with annoyance, Jill glanced briefly at David Melbury without shifting from her comfortable pose. "Perhaps it's because I'm always hoping not to be disturbed."

He nodded slowly, as though she had made a profound observation. "Perhaps." His sun-bleached hair was ruffled and his evening shirt open at the throat.

He came and leaned against the other side of the willow, joining Jill in her contemplation of the water, dappled, not by the moon, but by artificial stars, the tiny white lights strung around the outer perimeter of the gardens.

"I supposed you've noticed that my date has been chasing yours like a thing possessed all evening?" David suddenly said, without looking at her.

Jill also remained staring ahead. "I've noticed," she replied tranquilly.

"And you don't mind?"

"Not really. I hope she doesn't catch him but only because Chris deserves somebody much nicer than Sally."

David slowly turned his head so that he was looking at her across the brief space of the tree trunk. "He arrived here tonight with a much nicer person than Sally. He doesn't appear to appreciate his luck."

For a moment Jill didn't grasp what he had said. Then, when it dawned on her that he was talking about herself, her immediate reaction was one of suspicion; what was he up to? Was he piqued about Sally's interest in Chris, and trying to get his own back by paying attention to Jill? She frowned; it was terribly devious behaviour for such a warm night!

"What are you trying to say?" she asked, turning so that she could see his face. Their eyes met and she felt a tiny shiver of alarm as she read the message so clearly written in his. "Oh no! You said it yourself, I don't like you."

"But, Jill — " his voice was soft and persuasive — "you've never tried. I've always thought of you as one of the most interesting and attractive women I know, but for some reason, you took one look at me and decided that we wouldn't get on. What do I have to do to convince you otherwise?"

Jill turned to look for a way of escape but the stream was behind her and David in front; talk about the devil and the deep blue sea! "I'm convinced, David," she gabbled. "Now you must excuse me . . . "

But David had decided that she needed further convincing. As his arms closed about her Jill felt as though she was drowning; helpless and unable to stem the treachorous flood of feelings sweeping over her as David kissed her.

It crossed her mind that they might both have had too much to drink, but she had stayed within her own self-imposed limit for sobriety, and David appeared not to be displaying any signs of tipsiness — apart from his words and actions of the past few minutes. But it was not intoxication from the champagne which had thrown them together, but an attraction which she had sensed long ago but had never before acknowledged. An attraction which had scared her from the outset and made her shun him because she sensed that it could not lead to happiness.

They stepped apart and David was about to say something when a voice was heard sharply calling his name. He gave a soft, impatient groan and Jill seized the moment to turn and walk towards the house, her heart thudding painfully with her mixed emotions. There was a knot of people standing in the light streaming from the open windows of the ballroom, and she headed towards them, instinctively seeking company.

4

SALLY'S red-clad figure, turning and looking imperiously to see if David was obeying her summons, was prominent in the group; and one other, at the sight of whom Jill forgot her immediate problem and groaned aloud. Prue! What on earth was she doing here? As she drew closer she also recognised Chris, standing with his arm protectively draped across her cousin's shoulders. There were a couple of guests standing around, and three other teenagers, who were obviously with Prue.

"But, Sally, they're kids," Chris was protesting. "You can't call the police. They were just having a bit of fun gatecrashing a party."

"Trespassing," Sally contradicted him coldly. She looked over Jill's shoulder. "There you are, David. Come and deal with this. I found these scruffy urchins hanging about in the garden." She turned her cold gaze on Jill. "One of them claims to be related to you, Jill."

Under the circumstances Jill couldn't have been blamed if she had denied it, but one look at Prue's white, terrified face had Jill instantly leaping to her defence. "Yes, she's my cousin. I introduced her to you in the shop the other day." She was tempted to add, "but you were so concerned with buying those silly combs that you probably didn't take any notice," but that would only have made things worse.

"You can't possibly think this a matter for the police," Jill went on, trying to keep her tone reasonable. "You know Prue here, and Melanie, her parents are here tonight as your guests. And — " she looked at the two leather-clad youths and closed her mouth. She didn't know them and didn't want to. Where on earth had the girls found this pair?

"What do you think, David?" Sally drawled.

He looked baffled. "What's it got to do with me, Sally? Can't you or one of your staff deal with it? If you want my opinion I think you'd be going over the

229

top if you call the police, but it's entirely your business."

Jill stole a look at Prue's dismayed face as her idol rapidly developed feet of clay. Jill didn't blame him for maintaining a neutral attitude but Prue obviously saw it as an act of deepest betrayal in not leaping to her defence.

"Let's forget it, shall we?" Chris said reasonably. "There's no harm done. Come on, Jill, we'll take the girls home, and you two — " he gave each of the youths a poke in the chest — "push off before Mrs Crawshaw here does decide to let the law deal with you."

The two boys turned tail and ran down the drive towards the gate. Sally heaved an exaggerated sigh of relief and then gave an embarrassed laugh, as if she realised that she had over-reacted. "I'm sorry about that, everybody, but I get so nervous about that sort of thing now I'm all alone in this great big house."

'All alone except for the housekeeper, two maids and the live-in gardener,' Jill thought with unusual cynicism. Sally's last remark and her command for David to take charge of the situation were obviously broad hints to him that he should take charge of her life as well. But David was staring down at the gravel with a neutral expression which didn't bode well for Sally's ambitions.

Jill and Chris thanked Sally sincerely for a lovely evening and shepherded the chastened Prue and Melanie around to where Chris's car was parked. Jill noted with grim amusement that Prue was hanging tightly on to Chris's arm.

"What about your car, Jill?" Prue asked in a subdued voice as they started out for home. It was the first time she had spoken.

"What about it?" Jill asked tersely. "I hope it's not upside down in a ditch somewhere."

"No, it's over there." Prue pointed to the dark shape parked across the road from the drive.

"I'll walk up and fetch it in the morning, after you've told me exactly what tonight was all about. And you can write and apologise to Sally — I don't want her upset. She's quite capable of finding a loophole in my lease and throwing us both out into the street!"

231

After dropping Melanie home and shooing Prue upstairs to bed, Jill and Chris sat on the swing seat in her tiny back garden, talking over the evening.

"Whoever named your cousin Prudence was being optimistic rather than accurate," Chris said, chuckling. "Calamity Jane would be more appropriate."

"It's all David's fault. She probably only turned up hoping to see him." Jill declared. "He flirted with her when they first met, not realising how young she is, and she took him seriously. I think she's learnt her lesson — as far as David is concerned, at least. I'm a bit worried about the way she looked at you when you leapt to her defence. I think she now sees you as her new Mr Wonderful."

Chris made an expansive gesture. "And why not? She won't be the first."

Jill looked at his innocent profile with suspicion. When they first met she had taken such remarks at their face value, but the more she got to know Chris, the more she realised his outrageous comments were intended as self-mockery.

"It's a good job she didn't turn up ten minutes earlier and see you and him together," he went on drily. "And I hope Sally didn't see you either."

"It was nothing," Jill said guiltily. "I — er, I think he was a bit tight."

"He seemed sober enough to me — and so did you." He tried to look offended. "I'm deeply insulted; you turned quite nasty when I suggested doing exactly the same thing. What's he got that I haven't?"

"Nothing!" Jill said in exasperation. "I'm sorry, Chris, I thought we were just friends, not — well, you know. Besides, I don't care for David at all. He just sort of caught me off balance."

He gave her a disbelieving look. "Let me know next time it's going to happen and I'll make a point of being there to catch you myself."

Whether Prue overslept the following morning, or whether she was simply unwilling to face possible retribution was debatable, but she remained in her room until almost lunchtime. Jill was just taking the joint of roast lamb from the oven when Prue slipped into the kitchen and sat silently at the table, her head bowed.

In shame or penitence? Jill wondered. Or was it just an encore of a well-polished performance Aunt Hattie must have seen dozens of times: The Penitent Daughter or Oh, Mother, I'll Never Do It Again. But the tears in Prue's eyes were genuine, and they overflowed when Jill, cursing herself for being a softie, said, "Don't upset yourself over a silly prank, love. It really wasn't that dreadful."

"But it was," Prue sobbed. "I let you down so badly — and it wasn't my fault."

Jill frowned; she hadn't expected Prue to be so cowardly as to blame somebody else for her bad behaviour.

"Well, it was my fault in a way," Prue rushed on. "But I wouldn't have done it if it had been just me on my own"

"Tell me what happened," Jill said patiently. "Where did you and Melanie find those two young men you were with?"

Prue made use of a handful of paper hankies and then sat up and faced Jill squarely. "Keith and Roger? We met them at the dance. They're quite nice, really. Roger was a bit squiffy and didn't want to drive his car, so Mel and I offered to see them home in yours."

"Very liberated of you," Jill said drily. "Are they local boys?"

Prue nodded. "They come from the estate on the other side of the by-pass. Anyway, we had to go past the Crawshaw place, and Mel and I were moaning about not being invited to the party, so Roger said why didn't we invite ourselves."

She began to sniffle again. "It was only a bit of fun. We weren't going to burgle or vandalise the place, like Mrs Crawshaw seemed to think. We just — just . . . "

Jill's lips twitched. "You just wanted to see what the grownups were doing?"

Prue managed a watery smile. "Something like that. You won't send me home, will you, please, Jill?"

Jill felt a stab of surprise. There she was, thinking she was being hard on the girl, and Prue was worrying about being made to leave. "Of course not. You're the best assistant I've had for ages — and who's going to run the nearly-new stall at the jumble sale if you go?"

She was nearly strangled in a grateful hug. "Oh, bless you! Tell you what; I'll dress up all neat and respectable — perhaps you can lend me something — and I'll go and apologise to Mrs Crawshaw in person. How's that?"

"That's a super idea," Jill said. "But in future think before you act and you won't have to go grovelling to the people you've upset. And Sally was upset, you know."

"I know. I feel rather sorry for her," Prue said with a rare flash of adult insight. "I'll bet it's lonely for her in that big house all by herself. I'll take her some flowers."

"Don't overdo it," Jill was tempted to add, but Prue was obviously enjoying her slice of humble pie, so she held her tongue.

"Chris is awfully sweet, isn't he?" Prue remarked later, as they sat eating a belated lunch. "And terribly good looking. I suppose he's too old for me, as well?"

"Much too old," Jill said firmly, suppressing a groan. Had she been like this at Prue's age? If she had, her mother, whom she had loved dearly but had always regarded as being a perfectly ordinary woman, must have been a saint in disguise!

It was a very subdued Prudence who went about her work for the next few days; so subdued that Jill began to wonder exactly what Sally Crawshaw had said to the girl when she went to make her apologies for the gatecrashing incident. But when asked, Prue was reluctant to discuss it. "No, she was quite sweet in her own peculiar way," she denied, when Jill asked her if Sally had come down hard on her. "Said she understood. Promised she'd send me an invitation to her next party."

"Next year's ball?" Jill said. "That's a long way off. You might not still be here."

"No, not next year's ball!" Prue said vehemently. "Sally's engagement party. Didn't you know? She's going to marry David Melbury."

"Oh!" Jill said weakly. "I thought you'd got over him?"

"I have! I'm not worried about me. I was thinking about you. Or did you know about David and Sally before you let him make love to you on Saturday night?"

"Oh crikey," Jill murmured. First Chris remarking about it and now Prue. Why hadn't she and David simply put up a sign and sold tickets? She was more worried about the idea of being seen and gossiped about than she was by the news of David's duplicity.

"Aren't you upset by that double-crossing rat?" Prue demanded.

Jill shook her head and smiled faintly, unsure how to explain the pale greys of the situation to a girl who was still at an age where everything was seen in stark black and white. "Forget it, love. I have. It was just something that happened on the spur of the moment."

Prue wasn't satisfied. "You don't have to put a brave face on it on my account, Jill. I didn't realise there was anything between you and David. I can see now why you didn't like me fancying him, and why you pretended to dislike him. It must be awful, feeling how you do and knowing that he's going to marry Sally Crawshaw, and you having to keep the whole thing quiet."

"It isn't like that at all," Jill protested, her patience beginning to fray as Prue persisted in grasping the wrong end of the stick. "I don't especially like him and I certainly didn't know he was engaged."

And neither, she suspected, did David. He had looked annoyed rather than guilty when Sally's call for assistance interrupted their embrace on Saturday. Either Sally was taking David more seriously than he intended or she was simply indulging in wishful thinking. Oh well, it was none of Jill's business; she just hoped that David's behaviour towards her at the party was an impulse he would not repeat. And when Jill next saw David — she and Prue spent their afternoon off playing tennis at the club — his manner with her was so distant as to be out of sight, and she decided with relief that she was right; the events of Saturday night had been an aberration on his part and were not likely to be repeated.

5

JILL feared that the gatecrashing episode heralded an outbreak of the potential delinquency of which Prue had been accused by her mother, but it didn't materialise. Presumably rebellion was only possible where there was something against which to rebel, Jill decided with relief. She had given Prue more or less total freedom and, after carefully surveying the generous amount of rope, Prue had sensibly decided not to hang herself.

There was, in fact, Jill discovered as their intimacy grew, far more to her cousin than she had been led to believe. Beneath the careful pose of tough, streetwise teenager, Prue was a curious mixture of naivety and wisdom, cynical humour and sensitivity — and she had the kindest heart, which, although she didn't wear it on her sleeve, nevertheless attracted waifs, strays and deserving causes like a magnet.

As Mrs Protheroe's despair at not finding a volunteer fortune teller grew, Prue gamely offered to take on the task. Injured birds fluttered accurately into her path, flag sellers homed in on her like guided missiles; she was a sucker for a lame dog. Which was how they acquired Pooch.

"Can we keep him? He's only a baby," Prue pleaded.

Jill dubiously surveyed the bundle of black and white fluff Prue was clutching. Only a lolling pink tongue and furiously wagging tail betrayed the fact that it was a dog and not a grimy fur muff. "Old English sheepdog, isn't it? Don't they grow rather large to live in a flat?"

"He's only part sheepdog," Prue said defensively. "He's a mixture. There might be a bit of chihuahua there to counteract it."

"More like Shetland pony from the size of those paws. He's going to be enormous! Where did you find him? Are you sure he's a stray?"

It was Saturday morning. Prue had gone out to fetch their snack from the

241

patisserie. She had come back with two jam doughnuts and a very dirty puppy.

"There was a woman — I think she was a gypsy — selling things in the street. She was dragging the puppy around behind her on a piece of string. He looked so miserable, I offered her a fiver for him," Prue explained. "Please, please, Jill, may we keep him?"

Most people would have been content with a sprig of lucky white heather, Jill thought wryly. She lifted the tangled fringe of hair and met a pair of mournful brown eyes. It was the exact expression Chris assumed on the frequent occasions he accused Jill of sending him up.

"Very well, but he's your responsibility. You must see to his food and his visits to the vet for shots and things."

"I will, I will!" Prue squeaked delightedly. "You're an angel! Mother would never let me have my own dog, what with all her pedigree Siamese about the place. I'll go to the pet shop now and buy him a leash and his own dish and a flea collar."

Jill took a hasty step back. "Quite. What will you call him. I don't think he merits anything too posh; he's only a pooch."

"Pooch! I'll call him Pooch," Prue decided. "Poochi-Pooch," she crooned and the puppy licked her face in ecstasy at the unaccustomed attention and affection.

Jill smiled as Prue carried Pooch off to give him a much needed meal. It was obviously the beginning of a long and devoted love affair.

* * *

"Do you think it's sensible to let her keep Pooch?" Chris asked that evening as he and Jill sat in the restaurant at the country club. He had arrived to collect her and found the flat in chaos as the untrained puppy romped around, leaving a trail of devastation behind him. "Apart from the inconvenience now, you might be stuck with him when Prue goes home."

Jill bit her lip. "I hadn't thought of that and I don't expect Prue has. She seems to have become a permanent fixture, and there's no reason why she should

243

go home. She and I and her mother are quite happy with the arrangement. She's only been in Foxbridge for a few weeks but I'd miss her dreadfully if she did go."

Chris looked thoughtful. "Don't you like living alone?"

"I haven't thought about it much. I suppose not, although I've done quite a bit of it on and off."

"Have you ever thought of getting married?" he asked quietly.

Jill snatched up the menu and smiled at the waiter who had appeared providentially at their table. Chris's conversation generally had all the substance of candy floss and the sudden change confused and alarmed her. She had no objection to discussing such matters but not with Chris; that wasn't his role in her life. Going out with him was uncomplicated fun; she had thought that the feeling was mutual; it wasn't fair of him suddenly to turn all serious and reflective on her.

After they had ordered Jill sat back, ostensibly admiring the decor, in fact avoiding replying to Chris's question. Their surroundings were worth looking at. David had had the entire second floor of the Victorian building knocked into one enormous, airy room and furnished in keeping with the period. The heaviness of the reproduction oak furniture and brass fittings was offset by the ivory and pale aquamarine of the walls and soft furnishings. Long casement windows, open and framed with softly blowing curtains, looked out over the rolling Chilterns.

Jill recalled David asking her advice about the furnishings, and her somewhat brusque response: she was not an interior decorator. What was it about him that bothered her so much and made her unable to respond to him in a normal, friendly fashion?

As if providence had decided to give her another chance to find the answer, David chose that moment to enter the restaurant. Sally Crawshaw, in ice blue satin and a great deal of jewellery, was hanging on to his arm.

David caught Jill's eye, gave her a brief nod and began to steer Sally towards his reserved table. Unfortunately, before he could get her seated and distracted by the menu, she also spotted Jill — and Chris, bone-meltingly attractive in formal clothes.

"Hallo, darlings," she gushed, veering towards them with a reluctant David in tow. "How lovely! Might we join you?"

David bowed to the inevitable with a wry smile and beckoned a waiter to set two extra places. Chris also looked a little dubious about the arrangement, but Jill decided that, on the whole, it suited her. She could put up with David so long as they weren't alone; and Chris was in such a strange mood, company might turn him back into his usual uncomplicated self.

"How's little Patience?" Sally enquired of Jill.

"Prudence," Jill murmured.

"A sweet little girl," Sally chattered on. "Such a pity about all that . . . " She fluttered her hands around her own beautifully groomed hair and make-up.

Jill privately agreed but she wasn't having Sally rubbish Prue in company. "She's growing out of it, I think. We all go through weird phases at that age. Don't you remember, Sally, when we were about fifteen you fancied having a tattoo? A butterfly, if I recall, on . . . "

She stopped and sipped her wine, feeling that 'your ankle' would come as an anticlimax to Chris and David, who were goggle-eyed with curiosity.

Fortunately Sally took it in good part. "You are wicked, Jill, reminding me of my foolishness all those years ago. Golly, what a lot's happened since then!"

'To you, perhaps,' Jill reflected, 'but not to me.'

"Talking about our misguided youth," Sally went on. "Do you remember the crush you had on David? I mean, we were all potty about him but I think you were a hundred times more smitten than any of us. Honestly, David — " Sally turned to him with a giggle — "you were responsible for all the truancy in our school when one of your matches was on television."

Never had Jill longed so much for the ground to open up and swallow her. Sally wasn't deliberately being malicious; she didn't mind admitting her juvenile adoration of a tennis star, but Jill did — especially when he was sitting beside her!

David saw her embarrassment and came to her rescue. "As you said, we all go through strange phases at that age. Luckily most of us grow out of it."

Sally was not at all abashed. "What a pretty little thing!" she exclaimed, catching sight of the antique agate ring Jill was wearing on her right hand. "Is it yours or have you borrowed it from stock — I mean, is it for sale?"

Jill felt a sudden flash of distaste. Sally's own hands were weighed down with the precious stones Charley Crawshaw had lavished on her; diamonds flashed at her ears and around her neck, and yet she could still covet an inexpensive dress ring. Although, Jill noted, the only engagement ring Sally wore was the enormous diamond and sapphire creation with which she had, as a nineteen-year-old, dazzled her friends. Dire predictions had been made about her marriage to a forty-two-year-old widower but, despite all the theories that she had married him only for his money, Sally and Charley had appeared to be happy, and she was genuinely devastated by his sudden death.

Jill spread her hand and looked at

her own modest piece of jewellery. "It's mine. I've had it for years. It's an antique poison ring. Look — " she demonstrated the catch that flipped open the oval stone, revealing the tiny hollow beneath it.

"Good heavens, how fascinating," David murmured. He took Jill's hand in both of his and examined the ring closely. Her fingers, slim and tanned, with pearly pink nails, looked more than usually feminine lying in his broad palm. She was intensely conscious of the contact and only just managed not to snatch her hand away.

Sally was evidently aware of it too because she immediately turned to Chris, who had been strangely silent until now, and said, "I've bought myself a Porsche. Aren't I naughty, being so extravagant?"

Chris looked suitably impressed, and David was mercifully distracted from Jill's ring. Satisfied that the spotlight was now back on herself, Sally went on to describe her new four-wheeled wonder, rising admirably to the challenge of monopolising two very attractive men at the same time.

When they had finished their meal, and were sitting drinking coffee and idly talking, David proposed that they adjourn to the suite of rooms he occupied in the clubhouse.

"No, no," Sally interposed. "We'll go back to my place. I want to show off my new toy."

"Do we have to?" Chris murmured to Jill as they straggled across the car park. "The reflection from her jewellery is beginning to give me a headache."

Jill chuckled, relieved that Chris seemed more like his usual self. "I don't see how we can get out of it without being downright rude. Anyway, we've nothing better to do."

She didn't hear Chris's reply because Sally was now giving her orders about the travel arrangements for the two mile journey to her house. "I'll go with Chris in his dear little sports car. Jill, you don't mind going with David do you?"

'It's all the same if I do, isn't it?' Jill thought rebelliously, allowing David to hand her into his long white estate. I don't know what you're up to, Sally, but I'm getting too old for silly, manipulative games like this. If you want to play one man off against another, that's your business, but don't involve me.

"All right?" David asked as they pulled out of the car park and followed Chris's car along the winding lanes which led to the Crawshaw residence. "Don't let Sally upset you. She doesn't really have designs on Chris. She's getting back at me for something, I'm not sure what. It's a kind of game with her: 'I'm upset and you've got to guess why.'"

"Sounds awfully hard work," Jill said drily. "And I'm sure Chris can look after himself. I'd just rather have gone straight home. I'm sure my flat looks as though World War Three has broken out in it by now."

She made him laugh with a lively account of Pooch's adventures, and found herself wondering yet again why she felt so ambivalent about him. Right at that moment she could easily convince herself that he was the most charming man in the world. But the next time they met . . . She gave a mental shrug; there was no point in worrying about it.

Sally's house lay in a hollow and it was

only when they reached the rise which led down to the gates that they could see something was wrong. The lighting in the grounds had been augmented by a battery of headlights and several flashing blue beams.

"Oh, dear heaven, it's not a fire, is it?" Jill gasped in horror.

David accelerated, as did the sports car in front of them. "No, it's the police. I'd guess there's been a robbery."

His guess was right. They were met in the hall by a policeman who informed them that during Sally's and the housekeeper's absence thieves had expertly sabotaged the alarm system, tied up the two maids and made off with paintings, objets d'art and jewellery worth hundreds of thousands of pounds.

Jill, Chris and David waited awkwardly in the drawing room while Sally was questioned by the senior detectives.

"That was a Reynolds, wasn't it?" Chris said, pointing to a rectangular light patch on the wallpaper over the fireplace. "I was admiring it when we came here to the ball."

Jill nodded mutely, a little overcome

by the enormity of Sally's loss. She pointed to a glass display case, its lid standing open, its contents gone. "And that was Charley's collection of antique snuff boxes. He'd have been brokenhearted at losing them."

"Oh well," David said briskly, looking around the otherwise orderly room, "at least they seem to have been professionals. Amateurs would have vandalised the place as well. You must admit it's a nice, neat job."

Jill stared at him. "How can you say that? All Sally's beautiful things — gone. Most of it had been in the family for generations. And don't say they were insured — that's not the point."

David shrugged and dropped into an easy chair. "I'm just saying that they're only things. Sally should thank her lucky stars that nobody was hurt; she could have been here herself."

Just then Sally came into the room. Her rouge stood out in garish patches on her white face and she was only just hanging on her self-control. But good manners triumphed. "I'm so sorry to keep you all hanging around like this," she apologised, as though she had simply been called away to answer the door. "Haven't you helped yourselves to a drink?"

"We didn't like to," David said. "You know — fingerprints."

Sally made a dismissive gesture. "Oh, I shouldn't worry. The inspector seems to think that it was professionals who wouldn't be daft enough to leave any traces. Let's have a decent drink." She rustled over to the bell-pull and when the housekeeper appeared, said, "Pop down into the cellar, Mrs Wicks, and bring up a couple of bottles of that divine champagne — that's if those dreadful little men haven't stolen that as well! Honestly, I don't know what things are coming to."

Jill watched with admiration as Sally played the part of stiff-upper-lipped outrage to the hilt. She really was splendid, Jill thought, when you consider that, since Charlie's death, her 'things', as David had called them, were everything to her.

Chris was the first one to take his cue from Sally. "Champers!" he exclaimed.

"How marvellous! We'll drink to fame and fortune, or perhaps just fame, seeing as how you've lost a fortune."

"What do you mean: fame?" Sally asked.

"The newspapers will love it," Chris said. He sketched a headline in the air. "'Country House Theft; Beautiful Widow Robbed.' If I were you I'd sort out some glamorous photographs of yourself wearing the stolen jewellery. You'll make the front pages of the tabloids."

He had achieved his object; Sally was instantly distracted. "Do you think so? Golly, what fun!"

David responded to Chris's encouraging glance and added, "I'll ring my chums at the TV station; tell them to get a news team over here."

"You could announce a reward for the return of your property," Jill suggested.

Sally was entranced. She seized the champagne and poured it with a flourish into four tall, crystal glasses. "Make the most of a bad job, that's my motto. I'll probably go into shock when it finally dawns on me exactly what's happened, but for the moment — cheers."

They all drank and then Jill and Chris made their excuses to leave. David came to the door with Sally to see them off, and it crossed Jill's mind that he would probably remain there for the night.

"A gutsy lady that," Chris commented as they drove away. "She's gone up quite considerably in my estimation. Pity I can't say the same for her boy friend; a cold fish is how I'd describe David Melbury. A charming person like Sally deserves better"

Himself, perhaps? Jill wondered.

"How can you say that?" she argued contrarily. "You don't know him."

"Not as well as you, perhaps," he replied, giving her a quizzical sideways glance, "but enough to form an opinion. Oh, he's pleasant enough company but I can't imagine making a friend of him."

Jill wondered if he was jealous of David. It was an unlikely emotion in somebody who had as much going for him as Chris, but if he was attracted to Sally, who obviously preferred David . . .

They were silent for the remainder of the journey home, and, unusually, parted without making another date. Jill was a little hurt. She and Chris usually spent most of his weekends in Foxbridge together and she had come to regard him as her exclusive property.

6

THE following morning, while Prue was in the garden giving Pooch a much-needed bath, Poppy rang Jill to get a firsthand account of the robbery. As Chris had predicted, it featured largely in most newspapers and was, as Jill and Poppy laughingly agreed, the only time Foxbridge was likely to make front-page news.

"How are you and Chris getting along?" Poppy asked after they had exhausted the main topic.

Unseen, Jill pulled a pessimistic face. "OK, I suppose. I told you, we had dinner last night at the country club."

"Good, good. Well done," Poppy said in the tone doctors use when encouraging patients along the road to recovery. "I knew you two were made for each other."

"I'd hardly call it that," Jill denied truthfully. "We're friendly, nothing more. We see a lot of each other because Chris isn't here often enough to get to know anybody else. I think, after last night, Sally Crawshaw is much higher on his list of eligible local females than I am."

"Oh no!" Poppy was dismayed. "Anyone but Sally! Poor Chris; it will be like that dreadful Miranda business all over again. She almost broke his heart."

"Who's Miranda?" Jill asked, startled. Chris was the type to cause heart-break, not be the victim of it!

"She and Chris were going to be married — oh, a couple of years ago — but Miranda threw him over for some chinless wonder whose only attraction, as far as I could see, was that one day he'd inherit most of Shropshire. I can imagine Sally doing the same sort of thing. I mean, Miles says that Chris is destined for great things with the firm but he's only a junior executive at the moment — hardly in Sally's league."

"But Charley left Sally well provided for. Why should she want another wealthy husband?"

"Didn't you say she's just bought herself a Porsche? Her inheritance won't last long at the rate Sally spends," Poppy said shrewdly. "Chris might look divine and Sally might enjoy flirting with him but that's as far as it would go."

"Poor old love," Jill said, forgetting her slight attack of pique with Chris. "He must have some fatal attraction to gold-diggers. What was she like, this Miranda?"

"Gorgeous, though I hate to say so. All chestnut hair and long legs."

"Sounds like a racehorse to me," said Jill, who had taken an instant dislike to Miranda.

Poppy shrieked with laughter. "Come to think of it, she did have rather a lot of teeth. You won't mention her to Chris, will you? He's over her now but he was very upset at the time."

"Of course not."

When she had bidden Poppy farewell, Jill rang Keeper's Cottage and invited Chris to lunch. He accepted and she hung up in a glow of goodwill towards him. Poor Chris; he was far too nice to be the innocent victim of some spoilt little fortune hunter. On the other hand, it was reassuring to discover that physical perfection was no guarantee of happiness, and that even male chauvinists had vulnerabilities!

Prue, clad only in a swim suit and her personal stereo, had bathed Pooch and was endeavouring to catch and dry him. It was impossible to say which one of them was the wettest, and Jill laughed as she watch the puppy streak about the tiny walled garden with his dripping owner in frantic pursuit. "Why not just let him run about, the sun will soon dry him. I've invited Chris to lunch. He'll be here any time so you'd better go and clean yourself up."

With a wail of horror Prue dived indoors. She was just in time. The slam of the back door was echoed by a corresponding sound from Chris's car.

"You are idle," Jill chided him as he came in the side gate. "Fancy getting the car out to drive half a mile."

He grinned and fended off Pooch, whose affectionate greeting was threatening to drench his immaculate white shirt and cream slacks. "Rest and relaxation, that's why I come here at weekends. I get enough exercise rushing around all week."

"I don't think a hectic social life is

261

quite as beneficial as a good brisk walk," Jill countered.

Chris looked reproachful. "I don't know what you're implying but I meant work, and two evenings a week at my squash club."

She laughed and held up her hands in a gesture of peace. "Sorry, sorry, I'm sure you're a model of good behaviour."

"Besides," he went on, "I brought the car hoping you might like to go for a drive after lunch. Perhaps we could drop in and see how Sally's coping."

Alarm bells went off in Jill's brain as she recalled Poppy's warning and she was grateful that she could say truthfully, "I phoned her this morning to see if I could do anything, and she said she was going to spend the day in bed, recovering from the shock of the robbery."

Chris shrugged, thankfully not looking too disappointed. "Fair enough. Shall we have a run out to the Cotswolds, then, just the two of us?"

Jill nodded. "Lovely. A nice, peaceful afternoon in the country."

But when Prue heard of their plans she looked so disconsolate at being left on her own that Jill invited her to go with them. As she rushed off to change her outfit for the third time that day, Chris smiled. "I'm surprised she heard you. Doesn't she ever take those headphones off? How she listens to that rubbish all the time is beyond me; it all sounds the same to me."

"That's incipient old age," Jill teased him. "And it's not rubbish — Prue's discovered culture with a capital C. She came in the other night and caught me listening to Stravinsky. I expected a lot of ribbing about my taste in music but she sat and listened, and I've caught strains of all sorts of unlikely things leaking out of her earphones since then; Ravel and Debussy as well as Stravinsky."

"It sounds worth encouraging. That visiting Russian ballet company is doing Firebird as a farewell performance in a couple of weeks time when they get back to London from their tour and I was intending to go. Shall I try and get tickets for the three of us?"

Jill was taken aback by his generosity. "That would be wonderful. I'm sure Prue would love it — and I would too."

"Good, now, about this afternoon; perhaps we should take your car. It's going to be uncomfortable with four of us crammed in my car all afternoon."

Jill looked puzzled. "Four?" She followed Chris's gaze out of the window to where Pooch, now vastly improved in appearance, if not behaviour, was busily digging up her small lawn. "Oh crikey, I see what you mean. He's a lovable creature but we daren't leave him on his own for a second; he chews the furniture — and anything else he can get hold of. I'm wondering if I did the right thing in letting Prue keep him."

"Why did you?" Chris asked.

Jill remembered the big brown eyes which had looked at her so soulfully, and burst into laughter. "As a matter of fact, he reminded me of you."

He considered this with an expression that was comically rueful. "Should I be flattered or not? It's nice to know that you'd give me a home if ever I was down and out, but on the other hand, I've never seen myself as a pathetic stray."

Jill couldn't imagine Chris as a pathetic anything; she had difficulty even envisaging

264

Poppy's description of his state of distress after his broken engagement. Not that he was a cold or hard person, just the reverse, but he always seemed so cheerfully self-confident.

Perhaps, Jill reflected later as they meandered along the leafy lanes which led from one picturesque Cotswold village to another, he was just very good at playing the part he had decided most suited him; that of the fancy-free cynic and dilettante, collecting Victorian door knobs and lady's hearts with equal interest and ease. Perhaps he was more vulnerable than he appeared.

They did the statutory tour, taking in the major beauty spots, admiring the quaintness of everything and deploring the hordes of fellow tourists cluttering up the pavements and making parking impossible.

"Pooch and I will die of thirst if we don't soon have something to drink!" Prue declared dramatically from the back seat of the car as they crept through a tantalisingly pretty village; tantalising because they couldn't stop and look around, trapped as they were between two coaches, with not a parking space in sight.

As they ground to a complete halt Chris got out, saying to Jill, "Take over while I go and look for some refreshments."

She slid over behind the wheel and resumed their crawl. They reached the traffic lights at the end of the main street and Jill was wondering if she should drive around the block again when Chris rejoined them. He was carrying a plastic shopping bag which clinked refreshingly as he dumped it on the floor between his feet.

"Iced Pepsi for us and a bottle of Malvern water for Pooch," he announced.

Prue cheered from the back seat and Jill turned to give Chris a smile of thanks. Her attention was caught by a display of jugs in one of the many antique shops they had passed in the course of the afternoon. She didn't normally mix business with pleasure but one of her best customers had asked her to look out for a particular piece to add to his collection of commemorative pottery and it had become a question of professional pride for Jill to find it.

She couldn't see exactly what was in the window and her attention was diverted by the figure of a man who had just come out of the shop. His back was turned as he bent and locked the door behind him but there was something familiar about his bearing. Jill frowned as she waited for him to turn around; she was sure she knew him. Then she shrugged to herself; she must have seen him at one of the many sales she went to.

Prue had also spotted him. "Gosh, fancy opening up on a Sunday," she chortled. "I hope you're not getting any ideas about us doing that, Jill."

"What?" Jill wrenched her attention away from the antique shop and looked around at Prue. "Oh no, don't worry, I believe in having Sunday off."

They drove out of the village and parked in a lay-by next to a pleasant tract of common land. It was only when they were seated in the shade of an enormous oak, enjoying their cool drinks, and watching the puppy revelling in his freedom, that Jill recalled where she had seen the antique shop owner before. He was the white-haired man who had been in her shop the previous week; the man who had claimed to be Charley Crawshaw's chum from the army.

But he had stated quite definitely that, although he liked antiques, he knew nothing about them. So what was he doing owning — or even just running — an antique shop? Jill's face burned as she recalled her answers to the detective who had questioned her about Sally's burglary. No, she had assured him, she hadn't seen any suspicious strangers in town.

It was true. At the time the man hadn't been suspicious, just another browser who happened to be vaguely acquainted with a local family. His questions about the Crawshaw house and family must have been to ascertain that Sally still lived alone. It was only today, when Jill saw him locking the door of a business about which he professed to know nothing that he appeared suspicious.

"Oh, good grief." She rolled over in the grass and buried her face in her hands. "Oh no! I think I accidentally helped the people who burgled Sally's house."

★ ★ ★

"What am I going to do?" Jill mourned after she had explained the cause of her distress to Chris and Prue. "I feel like a criminal myself."

"No, no, don't be silly," Chris comforted her. "You weren't to know who the man was — even if he was one of the criminals, which we don't know for certain."

Jill got to her feet and brushed some loose blades of grass off her skirt. "Come on, I want to take another look at that antique shop."

She set out determinedly across the field to where the car was parked, her companions hurrying after her.

"What are you doing?" Chris protested in alarm. "Where are you going? You're not thinking of making a citizen's arrest, are you?"

Jill shepherded them into the car. "Of course not — he won't be there, you saw him leaving — but I want to be sure of my facts when I go to the police. I mean,

269

have you any idea what the village was called? And the name of the shop?"

Compton Bassett was the name on the signpost leading into the village, and Devereux Antiques was the shop. As it was early evening, the worst of the traffic was gone when they arrived back and Chris was able to park outside the darkened shop. The three of them stood with their noses pressed against the window, trying to see in.

"What are we looking for?" Chris said in exasperation. "If the man you saw was one of the thieves, he's hardly likely to be selling Sally's things in his own shop. The policeman I spoke to said that the stuff is probably on its way out of the country by now."

Jill turned and stared unseeingly across the street, heedless of the beauty of late afternoon sunshine bathing the old village in golden light. "I know," she muttered. "I haven't the faintest idea what I'm looking for. I just feel so responsible."

"That's absurd and you know it," Chris reasoned. "All you did was confirm that Sally lived alone except for the servants — he could have found that out from anybody, or from watching the house, which I expect he did anyway."

"I know, but if only I'd realised sooner that there was something suspicious about him I could have described him to the police on the night of the robbery. If he's the professional they think, they might have recognised his description and picked him up straight away. I mean, he's very striking. Poor Sally could have had all her pictures and jewellery back by now."

"And you might have the reward," Prue said practically. "Just think, ten thousand pounds; a new car, new clothes — wow!"

"Don't be so horribly mercenary," Jill said crossly. "I wouldn't accept it. If I'd been a bit more alert I'd have realised what the man was up to and there wouldn't have been any need for a reward in the first place."

She turned and gave one last despairing glance into the shop, as if hoping to see it suddenly full of Sally's stolen property, before getting into the car.

"I'll say one thing," Chris observed as he pulled away from the kerb. "Life in the country is far more exciting than I'd expected it to be. There was me wondering if it was going to be too quiet for me and I find I'm mixed up with a gang of international thieves."

Prue leaned forward, her elbows resting on the back of his seat. "If you think that's exciting just wait until next weekend and the annual church fete — now that really will be something!"

Despite it being Sunday evening they made their way straight to the police station. None of the detectives handling the robbery were on duty but Jill spoke to a young officer in uniform who appeared pleased by her modest information.

"Shall we call in and see Sally on the way home?" Jill said afterwards, forgetting her avowal to keep Chris and Sally apart. "It might cheer Sally up if she thinks there's a hope of getting her things back."

Sally was definitely in need of cheering up. The previous night's bravado, due mainly, Jill suspected, to excitement and champagne, had worn off and she looked very despondent as she greeted the three visitors. She was made-up as immaculately as ever but there was no disguising the dark circles beneath her pretty blue eyes.

"It's nice to see somebody sensible," she said as she led them through the house. "Everybody's been terribly sweet — I think half the town has phoned or called today, offering their sympathy — but I can only take so much. If one more person says to me: 'But you were insured, weren't you?' I shall scream. They seem to think I'm concerned only with the value of what's been stolen. But I keep thinking of how Charley would feel if he could see all the gaps on the walls and the empty display cases. We're sitting outside — it's so warm tonight, isn't it?"

So saying she led them out to the terrace, where David Melbury half rose from his cane chair to greet them.

Despite Sally's declared wish not to talk about the robbery, it was the inevitable topic of conversation, and Jill bravely confessed her small part in it.

Sally generously and sensibly poo-pooed the idea that Jill should bear any of the blame. "I think it was frightfully

273

clever of you to spot him today. Are you sure it was him?"

Jill pictured the upright figure and distinctive shock of white hair. "Positive. Funny thing, he doesn't look the criminal type."

David caught her eye and grinned. "I'm sure burglars don't all wear masks and striped jerseys." He stretched gracefully and suppressed a yawn. "I, for one, will be glad when the whole thing has blown over; we can get back to some normal conversation. What on earth did we talk about before the robbery?"

"Sorry if we're boring you, David," Sally said coldly. She turned to Chris. "You haven't had a chance to look over the house yet, have you? Come on, I'll give you the five bob tour; there's still some interesting bits and pieces left. Luckily the burglars didn't bring a furniture van with them."

When they had gone inside there was an awkward pause which Jill filled with a commonplace remark about the weather. She was, as always, vaguely uncomfortable in David's presence and was grateful for the presence of a third party. Then Prue, showing remarkable lack of timing, decided to go and see how Pooch was faring in the car, and Jill was left alone with David.

7

"YOU'RE always with Chris when I see you these days," David remarked as soon as he and Jill were alone.

It was a question rather than a statement and Jill felt obliged to explain. "He's a friend of friends. You know Poppy and Miles Hatherford, don't you? Chris works with Miles and rents Keeper's Cottage from him. I only see him when he's here at weekends." This sounded defensive and Jill, annoyed that David made her feel the need to justify her relationship with Chris, added, "I like him immensely; he's a poppet; very good company."

During this recital she was conscious of David's searching gaze and was grateful for the twilight. Where was Prue? And why was it taking Sally so long to show Chris around?

"I'm glad that you spend more time at the club these days," David said.

"Perhaps, if you come by yourself one evening, you'll have dinner with me?"

Jill looked up, surprised, and their gaze locked and deepened. She opened her mouth to refuse and, to her horror, heard herself saying, "Thank you, I'll think about it."

The whole sequence seemed to have been acted out in slow motion; then everything returned to normal speed as Chris and Sally emerged, laughing, from the house and Prue arrived back with Pooch panting and straining on his lead.

"Oh, what a little love!" Sally screeched, scooping up the wriggling bundle of black and white fur. "That's what I should have — a dog! You wouldn't have let the nasty men take Sally's precious things, would you?" she crooned to the ecstatic puppy.

"I told you to leave Pooch in the car," Jill said, confusion from her encounter with David making her voice sharper than she intended. "We don't want him digging up Sally's garden."

"He was bored," Prue protested. She made as though to rise and return Pooch to his former imprisonment. "But suit

277

yourself — he can chew another hole in the back seat of the car."

When they rose to leave shortly afterwards, David announced that he too must go; he had things to see about at the club. As they straggled around to where the cars were parked Jill was curious as to whether he would openly ask her to specify an evening for their dinner date but he didn't; he merely gave her a significant look during the general leave-taking.

His apparent wish for secrecy weighed heavily on Jill and made her even more determined to exercise her female prerogative to change her mind, and refuse should he renew his offer.

The following morning Jill was asked to return to the police station to confirm the identity of the suspected robber from a photograph they had on file.

"But why is it such an old photo?" she asked the detective. "He's aged quite a lot since this was taken."

He gave a wry smile. "Because we've only ever been able to put him away for one job, twelve years ago. He's clever, I doubt if we'll be able to tie him in with the Crawshaw case."

Jill was scandalized. "That's awful! There must be some way you can catch him."

The DI shrugged. "Innocent until proven guilty sometimes works in favour of the criminals. You'll see; we'll bring him in for questioning but I'll give odds on him having a glib explanation and a watertight alibi."

Jill fumed over the injustice of this all the way back to the shop, and Prue was equally indignant when given an account of the interview.

"Do you mean to say that he might get away with it?" she exploded. "After all the distress he's caused Mrs Crawshaw?"

"We don't know for certain he's guilty," Jill pointed out. "And fortunately for all of us, people in this country aren't locked up on purely circumstantial evidence. It's justice — no matter how unjust it seems."

"It's not right," Prue muttered. "There must be something somebody can do."

Jill was surprised at how badly the girl took the news. Then she reflected that it was probably the first real example Prue had had that life was not always fair, and that people didn't always get their just deserts, whether good or bad. At intervals throughout the day there were outbursts of protest from Prue, until Jill became quite exasperated. She had enough to think about without getting involved in arguments about the merits or otherwise of British justice.

She jumped every time the phone went in case it was David, ringing to pursue his invitation. Suppose she had another moment's aberration and said yes instead of no?

And the church fete loomed large. As the day approached the telephone wires between the committee members positively glowed with constant use as they made the final preparations.

If Jill had any doubts about her cousin's prowess as Madam Zara, as she had designated herself, Prue was supremely confident. With the help of her friend Melanie, who was a clever needlewoman, she had concocted a wondrous outfit out of a gauzy pink and silver sari which had turned up among the second hand clothing donated to the fete. Baggy harem trousers and a brief, fitted top were made and painstakingly decorated with sequins, beads and braid; masses of costume jewellery was borrowed, and a long dark wig was to cover Prue's own un-gipsylike locks.

Jill was delighted that she had been able, with perfect honesty, to send Prue's mother a glowing testimony to Prue's industry, good behaviour and evident desire to become a responsible member of society; about all of which Aunt Hattie had expressed grave doubts. Jill would have enjoyed taking the credit but she believed that the change in Prue had come about because of altered circumstances, rather than any individual influence.

And yet, Jill pondered as Prue slammed about the shop that afternoon, she was still capable of producing surprises. She had conformed to a point where she didn't turn heads in the street, without sacrificing any of her originality of self. She was still fresh and funny — and occasionally very irritating!

"Do stop crashing around like that," Jill complained. "Your breaking the stock won't catch Sally's burglars. Tell you what — pop upstairs and see if Pooch is all right. Take him for a walk if he seems to have chewed more of the furniture than usual."

When Prue had gone Jill got on with trying to catch up with her neglected bookwork. She was concentrating so hard that she didn't realise David had come in until he spoke to her.

"Hallo, Jill, you look lovely and cool on this hot day. Sorry," he added as she dropped her fountain pen and blotted the ledger lying open in front of her. "I frightened you."

'You usually do,' she was tempted to reply. Instead she replied with more coolness than she felt, "Hallo, David. I was so wrapped up in my work I didn't see you come in. I've got rather behind with my bookwork lately, what with the fete and everything, so I'm having a go at it now while it's quiet."

He failed to take the hint and made himself comfortable, leaning his elbows on the counter as though settling down for a long chat. "Now, about that dinner date I mentioned on Sunday night."

Jill took a deep breath. "No, thank you, David. I don't think so." There; she'd done it!

He looked taken aback. "Why not? I thought we were getting along better together these days. You disappoint me."

"Do I?" Jill said calmly. Her ability to refuse him had bolstered her confidence to the point where she felt able even to argue. "I can't think why. As you so often point out to me, we've never really got on together — why should we bother now?"

David looked genuinely taken aback. "Such hostility, Jill! What have I done to deserve it?"

"You aren't honest," she retorted. "If you were you wouldn't be so furtive in your approach to me. You must think I'm daft or blind — or both — not to have noticed. Can you not see that it's wrong to court Sally in public and me in private? She's an old friend of mine but even if she weren't, it would still be wrong."

David listened to this carefully. "So if I wasn't dating Sally, you'd be happy to go out with me?"

"I didn't say that! And how can you not go out with her? She told Prue that you and she were engaged."

He pulled a wry face. "Do we behave like an engaged couple?"

"No, I suppose not," Jill said reluctantly.

"Very well then. If that's your only objection, I'll stop seeing Sally."

Jill stared at him, aghast at the cold-bloodedness of his suggestion. "But it doesn't work like that, David. Sally and I are people, not library books that you can exchange when you feel like it. There are feelings involved."

"I realise that. I'm sorry, Jill, I expressed myself badly. Look," he went on in a reasonable tone of voice. "Sally and I are not engaged or in love or anything like that. I would have thought it was obvious."

"To you, perhaps. What about Sally?"

He shrugged. "I have the impression she's rather keen on your chum Chris."

"Oh dear," Jill murmured. "It's beginning to sound like a bad soap opera. You know — Sally is attracted to Chris, who goes out with Jill, who is fancied by Sally's boy friend, David . . . "

284

And to think that a few weeks ago she had been sitting upstairs with Poppy, bemoaning her dull life!

"Well?" David encouraged her. "Have you changed your mind?"

She shook her head decisively. "Sorry, David. It's not just because of Sally; it wouldn't work. There's no common ground between us."

He banged the heel of his hand down on the counter, making both Jill and her ledger jump. "You can't dismiss it just like that, Jill; you can't! You're being unreasonable. This isn't just a whim on my part. Ever since I moved here I've been trying to get to know you. I've watched you and admired you — and wondered what I've done to make you snub me."

He paused, seeming to want an answer. Jill didn't have one and stared unhappily down at the counter as he continued, "I thought, recently, that we were beginning to . . . That we might . . . "

A lesser woman might have felt triumph at the sight of the idol of her teenage years standing before her, pleading and stammering like an adolescent. Jill could feel only misery.

He was watching her with the intensity which always discomfited her and she shivered, her cotton sundress suddenly too cool for the shadowed interior of the shop. David's unwavering gaze was making her conscious of her bare shoulders, and she felt a claustrophobic urge to run out into the sunlit street and seek safety among the shoppers thronging the pavement.

Her voice caught in her throat and she had to swallow before saying, "Please leave me alone, David."

He drew in a sharp breath and for one awful moment she thought he was going to argue. But he merely said, "For now, Jill, but I'll be back."

She had only a couple of minutes to brood over this disturbing encounter and then Prue burst into the shop, with Pooch straining on his lead in one hand, two dripping ice cream cornets in the other, and provided a merciful distraction.

★ ★ ★

286

There was no dramatic news of an arrest in the Crawshaw robbery case so presumably Dennis Murdoch had proved to be as slippery a fish as the detective predicted. It rankled with Jill but she resolved to worry about it, and her problem with David, when she had more time to do so. But for the remainder of the week her energy and thoughts were devoted to next Monday's fete.

The main talking point among those involved was: would the beautiful weather last? For nearly a month there had been a heatwave, interrupted only by a few overnight showers. It had to end sometime and pessimists were predicting that it would do so over the Bank Holiday weekend. Knowing the British weather's ability to spring nasty surprises, the fete organisers scanned the cloudless blue skies with apprehension. Should they put the whole thing under canvas and have done with it?

Prue had been in a strange mood all week. There was an air of fervid excitement about her which made Jill nervous; it was like living with a smoking volcano. Playing the role of Madam Zara

287

wasn't so thrilling as to cause Prue to behave like a hyperactive Jack-in-a-box, and Jill wondered what the other reasons could be. Perhaps Prue had a romantic attachment she was keeping secret.

If this was so, it was untypical — she usually treated Jill to a blow-by-blow account of her dates. Not that there had been many; Melanie was her usual companion. Roger, her accomplice at the gatecrashing incident, had made one more appearance before being cast aside in favour of Nicholas, whose father owned the riding school.

Apart from these two — and the occasional passing fancy for somebody totally unsuitable, like David — Prue showed a healthy impatience with the opposite sex, and Jill wondered what other reason there could be for her odd behaviour. But she had learnt that the surest way of turning Prue into a Sphinx was to question her about her activities, so she kept quiet and waited; all would be revealed in the end.

On Sunday afternoon Jill was relaxing after lunch with the papers while Prue got ready to go out.

"Oh, you look really terrific!" she exclaimed with pleasure when Prue presented herself for inspection. She was wearing matching cropped pants and voluminous shirt in white cotton splashed with vivid primary colours. Her fashionable make-up was subtle and her hair had grown sufficiently for it to curl softly about her delicate face and neck.

"Going somewhere special?" Jill asked casually.

Prue shrugged. "Out and about — you know — with a chum."

Jill gave a secret sigh of relief. Melanie, a year older and wiser than Prue, would keep her out of mischief. "Well, make sure you've got your key and don't be too late in."

Prue relented a little. "I never am, am I?. Don't worry. Are you going out?"

"I thought I'd pay a few calls. I'll have to take Pooch with me."

Her cousin sniggered. "That should make you unpopular around the neighbourhood."

Jill, dressed comfortably but prettily in a pale jade cotton sundress, dropped in on two old school friends and her godmother. By the time she reached her final destination, Keeper's Cottage, she was awash with tea, goodwill and gossip.

Chris was not, as she had expected, lounging idly in the hammock with a book, but gardening. She stood at the gate for several moments watching with surprise and amusement as he attacked the overgrown borders, enthusiastically uprooting dandelions and ripping bindweed from the hollyhocks. He was wearing only a pair of faded old jeans and Jill wondered how he had acquired such a marvellous physique sitting behind a desk all day.

Then Pooch barked as he recognised Chris, and Jill hastily opened the gate so that he wouldn't think she had been standing admiring him.

"What's all this?" she said, laughing at him as he came to greet her. "This is hardly the rest and relaxation you come here for."

"Guilt, I'm afraid. I saw Miles' mother in town in the week and she asked me how the garden was looking. 'Like a jungle' wouldn't have pleased her so I thought I'd better tidy it up before she comes to look for herself."

"I should think so," Jill said. "That garden was Beatrice's pride and joy. But I think it would be easier if you got a gardener. Do you want me to try and find somebody who can do a few hours each week, just to keep it looking civilised?"

"Would you? I don't spend enough time here to cope with it. Look — " he held out his usually well groomed hands, now encrusted with greyish mud — "I don't think I'll ever get my nails clean, and the blisters!"

"Aah," she crooned unsympathetically. "Never mind, you're still a thing of beauty — or you will be when you've showered."

"I'm surprised you've noticed," he pretended to grumble as they strolled along the brick path towards the cottage. "I thought you only had eyes for blond ex-tennis champions. Be a love and make some tea while I clean up, will you?"

As Jill pottered about the kitchen, making tea and slicing a fresh cream sponge cake she found in the fridge, she mulled over Chris's words with disquiet.

Was the reluctant fascination she felt for David Melbury so obvious? And how had she let it get so out of hand?

"Cheer up, angel," Chris said, coming into the kitchen, bathed, shaved and elegant in pearly grey slacks and shirt. "I've got those tickets for the ballet. Next Friday at Sadlers Wells. It'll seem odd, seeing you in town on a weekday. I always think of you as my weekend-in-the-country girl."

"I'll try and make sure there isn't any straw sticking out of my hair," she said drily. "What are your weekday-in-town girls like?"

He rolled his eyes expressively. "Gorgeous — but not a patch on you. Where's the ill-named Prudence today?"

Jill frowned as they carried the tea things out to where a table and chairs stood in the shade of a chestnut tree. "Why do you call her that? You sound like Aunt Hattie."

Chris concentrated on setting out the cups. "Oh, no reason."

"Yes, there is," Jill persisted. "You must have a reason."

He pulled a face. "I saw her earlier

292

this afternoon; she went past here with a chap in a beat up old car."

Jill bit her lip. "She gave me the impression she was going out with Melanie. I suppose she's got a new boy friend. She's nearly eighteen, Chris. I can't be expected to know her every movement. Besides, it was probably that nice Nicholas Winters."

"This chap didn't look like that nice anybody — he looked most un-nice from what I saw of him; only young but rather unsavoury and spivvy. Perhaps I'm wrong, perhaps that's the latest fashion but I don't think so."

"Oh dear. I don't usually ask Prue where she's been or with whom, except in a friendly sort of way," Jill said worriedly, "but I think I should tonight. She won't like it, I know she won't."

Prue didn't like it, not one little bit.

"I don't ask you where you've been," she said childishly, when Jill questioned her on arrival home that night. "It's only ten o'clock, I'm sober and in one piece; what more do you want?"

She had a point and Jill wondered if she should drop the matter. But Prue was still wearing the same air of suppressed excitement which had made Jill uneasy all week, and she persisted, "Why are you being so secretive, Prue? I'm not prying, honestly, but I do feel responsible for you. If you've nothing to hide why won't you say where you've been and with whom?"

"All right, I've been out for a drive and a drink — one drink — with a friend. His name's Tony; you don't know him. OK?"

"OK. What's he like, this Tony?" Jill asked with a great deal more benevolence than she was feeling.

They were in Prue's room and Prue was prowling around, fidgeting with the litter of make-up and clothes lying about, so that she wouldn't have to meet Jill's eyes.

"I mean," she went on in the same mild tone, "what does he do for a living; how old is he?"

"For heaven's sake, Jill!" Prue slammed shut the dressing table drawer. "You sound just like my mother! I thought you were different, I really did. Please believe me, I'm not doing anything shameful or wrong."

And Jill had to be content with that. She knew if she persisted with her questioning it would precipitate a row. And, on the face of it, Prue was doing nothing wrong. She was dating a young man and, as teenagers frequently do, wanted to make a little mystery out of it.

But Jill kept seeing her cousin's abnormally bright eyes and secretive smile. Chris, the most tolerant of mortals, had referred to this Tony person as 'unsavoury and spivvy'. It was very worrying and Jill lay awake for a long time, wondering how to handle the problem. To telephone Aunt Hattie for advice would be an admission of failure, and would probably bring her tearing up from Brighton, breathing hell-fire and prophesying all kinds of bad ends for both of them!

When she rose in the morning Jill still wasn't certain what attitude she should take towards Prue. Should she pretend that all was forgotten, or maintain her air of disapprobation?

In all events, the problem was solved for her. When she went into Prue's room at nine o'clock to wake her with a cup of tea, she found the bed empty except for a note lying forlornly on the pillow. Prue had at last lived up to her reputation as a runaway.

8

"I DON'T think you should upset yourself about it too much," Chris said. "After all, she doesn't say she's running away, just that she's gone out and you're to expect her when you see her."

They were sitting in the kitchen of Keeper's Cottage, a hastily brewed pot of coffee on the table between them. Upon finding Prue gone, Jill, at a loss what to do, rang Chris for his advice.

"I've only just got up. Why don't you pop over and we'll talk about it over breakfast," he had invited her.

Jill perused the note again. 'Dear Jill, As you can see I've gone out. I can't tell you when I'll be back because I don't know. I would have explained last night but you might have asked more awkward questions. I could be gone some time — if I'm not back for the fete, I hope my Madam Zara costume will fit somebody else. Love, Prue.'

"She sounds reproachful rather than angry," Jill said unhappily, "as though it's my fault instead of hers. Oh, I could strangle her, really I could! Where can she be?"

"Wherever she's gone must be pretty important for her to pass up her chance of playing at fortune teller," Chris mused. "She's been looking forward to it so much. Didn't you get any hint last night what she's up to? What about this Tony fellow?"

"She refused to discuss him — said I was carrying on like her mother," Jill replied, upset not just because Prue had mysteriously vanished, but because she, Jill, might have driven her away.

"Hey — " Chris took her hand across the small table — "it's no good you feeling guilty, angel. It's obvious that she was intending to go, with or without your knowledge and blessing."

"You honestly don't think I upset her so much she's run away?" Jill asked hopefully.

He smiled at her with gentle exasperation. "Don't be an ass. Of course you didn't. She wouldn't run off leaving all her clothes and things — and her pesky puppy — now would she? Come here."

He got up and, coming around to her side of the table, pulled her up into his arms, gently rocking her as though she were a child in need of comfort. Jill rested against him and closed her eyes. She couldn't remember the last time she had leaned on somebody, either physically or emotionally; it was so lovely and soothing.

Chris suddenly let her go and began briskly to clear the table. "So," he said cheerfully, "I think you should stop worrying and concentrate on enjoying yourself at the fete this afternoon. Heaven knows you've worked hard enough to make it a success."

"Enjoy myself?" Jill echoed incredulously. "I suppose you realise that, with Prue missing, the hunt for a fortune teller has to begin all over again — and with only a few hours to go! I wish Mrs Protheroe had never thought of it. She should be made to do it herself."

Chris snorted with laughter. "From what I've seen of her, she'd have a job getting into Prue's skimpy outfit. You could, though. I'll lay odds that you end up crouched over the crystal ball this afternoon."

Chris was right. A replacement for Prue couldn't be found, and Jill, guilty that her cousin had precipitated the crisis, stepped in. She handed over the bric-a-brac stall, its contents safely evaluated, to the vicar's sister.

Chris wasn't entirely right about the costume fitting Jill. It did after a fashion, but the brief top and low-slung harem pants had been tailored for Prue's boyish figure. As Jill changed into them in the spare bedroom at the Vicarage, she was alarmed at the strain being put on the seams, and the amount of bare flesh on view.

"I can't go out in public looking like this," she protested to Mrs Protheroe, who was hovering around her with a handful of safety pins, reinforcing the most likely breaking points "It's indecent and it's giving me bulges in the most peculiar places."

"Nonsense," said Mrs Protheroe bracingly. "It's most becoming — very glamorous." This reassurance was some-what nullified when she added, "And with the wig and veil nobody will recognise you anyway."

Jill was taking no chances on that. After fitting the long black wig over her own tied-back hair, she circled her eyes with thick lines of kohl and applied so much mascara she felt as though she was peering through prison bars. Then, taking refuge in a raincoat, which, in the sultry heat, looked almost as outlandish as the costume, she went with her fellow committee members to inspect the troops.

Farthing Meadow, decked en fete, was a glorious sight. The freshly-mown, greeny-gold turf was edged on all sides with a creamy ruffle of cow parsley. On one side lay the church and its grounds through which entrance to the fete was gained; and adjoining that was another field, its silvery grass scarcely rippling in the still heat of early afternoon. The other two sides of the meadow were bordered by a small beech wood; and the marquees, always heat traps, had been set up in what shade it afforded.

Even as Jill and her companions walked around, enjoying the peaceful scene, the first visitors began to arrive, paying their entrance fees and standing about waiting for the local celebrity who was opening the fete.

Last year it had been David Melbury. This year it was to be Colonel Humphrey Bellingham, who successfully wrote lurid crime fiction under the pen name of Eleanor Wyndlesham, on the shaky theory that the public expected detective novels to be written by women.

"Jill?" Chris appeared at her side, looking breathtakingly attractive in palest blue and attracting many wistful feminine glances. "Is that really you, angel, behind all that hair and make-up? No wonder I couldn't find you straight away. Well, come on, let's have a look at the rest of the outfit."

Jill clutched her raincoat tightly about herself in an agony of embarrassment. "I'd rather you didn't. I feel as though I'm having one of those awful dreams, where you're walking along a crowded street wearing just your undies. I'm not taking my mac off until I'm in the tent."

She put on her head-dress, a silver

pillbox hat trimmed with tiny bells, and adjusted the veil across her face. "There. Do you think anybody will recognise me?"

Chris studied her carefully, noting the real anxiety in her lovely grey eyes, and solemnly shook his dark head. "No. They'll all think it's Hedy Lamarr."

She could tell he was dying to laugh and, as they made their way to her tent, blessed him for not doing so.

It was a neat little blue and white striped affair, with an eye-catching, crescent-shaped sign hanging over the entrance proclaiming: Madam Zara, Fortune Teller. The Arabic style lettering was embellished with stars and planets. Prue had designed and made it herself.

A sudden wave of fear for Prue washed over Jill, and Chris stopped laughing as he saw her eyes fill with tears.

"This is no way to carry on, Madam Zara," he murmured. "She'll turn up, don't worry. And for heaven's sake don't cry — it'll take you hours to clean up your face if all that mascara starts to run."

Jill managed a wobbly giggle. He gave

303

her a consoling hug and, lifting her veil, dropped a kiss on her cheek before pushing her gently towards the tent. "Go on, get your crystal ball polished up before the punters start queuing."

Fortune telling was, Jill mused, an hour later, money for old rope. Hope was the key to successful prediction; tell miserable people that they will be happier; tell happy people that things will get even better. So far nobody had appeared to take her seriously but, just in case, she had kept her predictions very general; no rash forecasts of spectacular wins on the premium bonds, or promises of dark, handsome strangers looming on the horizon.

Sally Crawshaw was a visitor, her white linen suit and cartwheel straw hat the antithesis of Jill's exotic inelegance. But Sally was bearing a tall glass of iced lemonade which banished any resentment Jill might have felt at the comparison between them.

"You poor old love. I thought you could use this," Sally drawled, plonking herself down in the chair on the opposite side of the small cane table which bore all the paraphernalia of Madam Zara's mystic arts. "What a rotten job to be stuck with on a day like this. I just saw Prue's little chum carting that adorable puppy about and she told me what's happened. Fancy Prue pushing off like that. Typical of kids today — no sense of responsibility."

It was too hot to argue and Jill was inclined to agree with Sally anyway, although she wasn't so disloyal as to admit it.

Sally removed her hat and fanned herself with it. "How can you bear it in here? It's like a sauna."

Then she leaned forward confidentially and Jill learned the true purpose of her visit. "Word is that you're frightfully good at this fortune telling business and — well, sweetie, I've got this little problem with my love life you might help me sort out. You know — help me make a decision."

Jill stifled an impatient sigh. Surely nobody, not even Sally, was so gullible as to believe anything told to them by Madam Zara?

"It's just a bit of fun to raise money

for charity," she pointed out. "I'm not a real fortune teller — or an agony aunt either, come to that."

Sally giggled. "I suppose not. Oh well, I'll tell you anyway. You see, I don't know what to do about David. I mean, I thought we were perfect for each other but then, when I met Chris — he's so sweet and scrumptious . . . At first I just made a play for him to make David jealous . . . You don't mind me talking like this, do you? I know you and he are just chums."

Jill politely tried not to fidget as Sally described her predicament. Had she ever felt so hot and uncomfortable? She let Sally waffle on for another minute and then said firmly, "I think you should do exactly what suits you, Sally."

After all, it was the policy Sally had successfully pursued all her life. And Jill reckoned that David and Chris were sufficiently adult to cope with whatever decision she reached.

Sally brightened. "Do you think so? Yes, you're right! I will." She planted her hat firmly on her head, dropped a fiver in the bowl of contributions and

306

vanished, leaving Jill wild with curiosity as to Sally's intentions.

The afternoon seemed interminable. Chris popped in several times with refreshments, encouragement and progress reports. It all sounded great fun and Jill was very tempted when, after glancing at the bowlful of money she had collected, and at her hot, tired face, he said, "Why don't you call it a day, Jill? Go and change and we'll enjoy what's left of the afternoon together."

She had bought a cool, ice pink cotton dress for the occasion. To slip into it and spend the rest of the afternoon with an amusing companion like Chris would be bliss, but she resisted. If she relaxed now she would start worrying about Prue.

"There's no sign of her, I suppose?" she asked for the umpteenth time.

And he replied, as he had done on the previous occasions, "No, but don't worry — I'm sure she'll turn up safe and sound. Now, are you sure you want to carry on here?"

"Just half an hour longer."

It was a decision she immediately regretted when Chris's place was taken

307

by David. "I'm just closing," she snapped as he seated himself opposite her. "I'm all out of predictions and patience."

Her shortness with him was partly because she was hot and tired but mostly because she had subconsciously been expecting and dreading his visit all afternoon. It said much for his tolerance that he replied evenly, "I'm not surprised. You deserve a medal for sticking it for so long. Are you sure you can't manage one more consultation?"

Jill had a nasty idea what it was going to be about. Oh well, she might as well face him now and have done with it. This was well on its way to being one of the worst days of her life. "What do you want to know?"

His blue eyes were serious as they met hers. "I want to know, once and for all, Jill, do I stand a chance with you; any chance whatsoever? If you say no I won't ever mention it again."

She looked down and wasn't surprised to find her hands knotted together in her lap. Pictures danced through her mind; of a summer long past when David had been the golden idol of her youth;

of the way his presence in Foxbridge had mocked and disturbed her; of their passionate embrace at Sally's ball.

He sensed her reluctance to banish him finally from her life and went on persuasively, "I'm not talking about an affair. Jill. I'm talking about much more than that — our lives, possibly. We could mean so much to each other, I'm certain. Please, it's important that I have an answer now."

'This is not fair,' Jill thought in agony. 'How can I deal with this with any dignity, when I'm hot, sticky and dressed like a third-rate stripper?'

"I thought — for a while — after my accident," David went on, "that I'd never feel any positive emotions again. I didn't even try. They shot the horse, you know, because his leg was all smashed up." His mouth twisted wryly. "Nobody offered to do me the same favour. Oh, I got over it after a fashion — life goes on and all that — but it wasn't until I got to know you better that I felt really alive again, the way I did ten years ago."

"Believe me, Jill," he pleaded, "I wasn't any happier about it than you were.

I'd got used to the way I was; I felt comfortable with it. I tried to ignore my feelings but . . . Please, say something."

Very few women are offered the chance of giving a man back his lost youth and hope, and if Jill had been more vain or less sensitive she would have been tempted to accept. As it was she could only shake her head, afraid to speak in case she replied with her emotions rather than her common sense. Pity was no substitute for love, and physical attraction was a transient thing; without genuine feeling to back it up it was falsely glittering and worthless.

"Jill?"

David's voice broke through her reverie and she registered the muffled sounds outside the tent; children's shrieks and giggles, disjointed snatches of conversation as people drifted past.

"I'm sorry, David, truly sorry," she choked, "but it wouldn't work, you must see that. I wish I could say it would but I can't."

Her eyes pleaded with him to understand. He nodded as if he, too, was unable to speak clearly. His hand briefly touched hers and then he was gone, leaving Jill fighting back the storm of sobs that was clogging her throat.

She stumbled blindly to the entrance and hung up her 'Back in 10 minutes' notice. Then she sat down, put her head in her hands and wept. There was no one reason for her tears, just an accumulation of misery and guilt which had built up over the day. Worry about Prue and the necessity of playing a part which was alien to her mood had already given the afternoon a nightmarish sense of unreality, and the scene with David had been the last straw.

Under normal circumstances Jill's unhappiness might have been tempered with a healthy dose of anger at his persistence but so low did she feel that she was overcome with sorrow.

Poor David — and poor Jill, to be made to feel responsible for blighting his life for a second time. And how could he be so thoughtless as suddenly to reveal that he was a normal human being rather than the cool, heartless creature she had supposed him to be?

"Jill!" Chris came dashing into the tent.

He paused when he saw her hunched, crying figure and then, with a muffled curse, came and crouched beside her. "Oh, angel, please don't. I saw him come in here and knew that something was wrong. He's not worth it."

Jill turned her head away, partly because she didn't want to speak and partly because she was conscious of rivers of mascara flooding down her face. Chris thrust a large white handkerchief into her hands and while she mopped her face and fought for control, he paced about, his long legs covering the small space with three strides each way.

"I could see this coming," he muttered, half to himself. "I knew he'd cause you grief; he's cold, arrogant and selfish."

"But he's not!" Jill wailed. Half an hour ago she would have agreed but that was before she glimpsed the more vulnerable side of David Melbury. "David's not like that, not deep down."

Chris gave a deep sigh and threw his arms wide in a gesture of exasperation. "Don't tell me — nobody understands him but you."

"That's right!" Jill snapped, nettled by

his sarcastic tone. She finished wiping her face and sat upright, her whole attitude defying Chris to continue meddling in her business. His hankie looked as though she had blacked her boots with it and she tucked it out of sight beneath the cushion on her chair.

"Women!" Chris exclaimed. "I will never, if I live to be ninety, understand them. How could you possibly think of throwing yourself away on a shallow character like David. Surely, as an intelligent woman, you can see that he'd have made you utterly miserable?"

"What's it got to do with you?" Jill yelled. "I shall throw myself away on whomsoever I like. If I want to throw myself away on David Melbury, I will!"

"Over Sally's dead body," Chris said grimly. "She was telling me, not half an hour ago, that she's decided to marry him."

Jill sat down, deflated. "Oh." Then she recovered her dignity. "Sally's always saying that she and David are engaged. It means nothing. It's just wishful thinking."

Chris shrugged. "She seemed pretty

convinced of it to me. She said that she'd become tired of shilly-shallying around and that she'd asked him to marry her."

And David had come to discover Jill's feelings towards him before making a decision. But how awful for Sally, was Jill's first reaction; to be dependent on another woman's answer before receiving one yourself. Sally must never know; and nobody who might tell her must know either. If Chris chose to believe that Jill was upset because David had just broken the news of his engagement, then so be it. It could make no difference to their friendly relationship.

"Oh well," she said with what she hoped looked like a brave smile, "let's not make it a reason for us to quarrel. I'm sure it's for the best. It's what Sally's wanted ever since she clapped eyes on David."

"By the way," she continued, hoping to change the subject. "Why did you come dashing in here as though there was a fire?"

Chris slapped his forehead with the heel of his hand. "Good grief, I'd almost forgotten! Good news. The wanderer's returned."

"Prue? But that's marvellous! Is she all right? Where has she been?" Jill's previous misery fled like mist before a fresh breeze. She pulled on her raincoat over her costume and impatiently tugged Chris's arm. "Come on. Where is she?"

She stopped outside the tent, blinking, dazzled by the dull red sun hanging low in the sky. No wonder it was so humid; great inky storm clouds were piling up on the eastern horizon and the light had a curious yellow glare.

"She's over there," Chris said, pointing to where a familiar, brightly clad figure stood by the entrance.

Jill began to hurry and then forced herself to adopt a normal pace. "Hi," she casually greeted her cousin, "You missed a lot of fun this afternoon. Look at me — " she indicated her appearance, forcing a merriment she didn't feel — "Madam Zara, the world's worst dressed fortune teller. Did you have a nice day?"

Prue nodded. "Sort of. Look, Jill, I'm sorry I let you and the committee down but I had something important to do I . . . "

"That's all right," Jill interrupted. Although burning with curiosity, the last thing she wanted was for Prue to feel obliged to explain. Her taunt about Jill behaving like her mother had struck home. "It's none of my business. As you said last night, you're nearly eighteen; what you do is your own responsibility . . . "

By now Prue was almost hopping about with impatience. "But I want to tell you!" she exclaimed. "I feel so bad about being secretive but if you'd known what I was up to you'd have gone raving mad."

A few coin-size spots of rain fell and the limp bunting fluttered to life as a fresh breeze swept across the fields. Jill shivered and hugged her coat about her, chilled more by Prue's words that the change in the weather. "I think we'd better get under cover or we'll all be soaked."

She looked around, as though slightly bewildered, and allowed Chris to shepherd them into a deserted tent.

"Look." Prue delved in her white shoulder bag. "I bought this this afternoon."

It was a silver snuff box with a jewelled and enamelled lid. Jill turned the small, brilliant object over in her hands, puzzled by its familiarity. "But why, Prue? And how could you afford it? It's Fabergé — not priceless but unique and worth a darn sight more than you can afford. And why should you want it?"

Prue sighed and rolled her eyes, the way she did when Pooch was being more obstinate or stupid than usual. Chris took the snuff box from Jill and examined it. "It's part of the Crawshaw collection, isn't it? I recognise its description from the list the police left in your shop, Jill. What have you been doing, young Prudence? Not living up to your name, I'll be bound!"

By the early hours of the following morning Jill began to wonder when she had ever been so tired. During the day of the fete she had been subjected to almost every possible human emotion; on top of that she and Chris had spent a couple of hours waiting at the police station while

317

Prue explained her actions and made a statement which, hopefully, would bring the perpetrators of the Crawshaw robbery to justice. And then, on the way home, Prue had demanded that she be allowed to call on Sally and give her the good news.

This was where they now were, lounging in Sally's elegant drawing room, drinking champagne and talking. The occasion was, in fact, a double celebration; the possible recovery of Sally's treasures, and her engagement to David.

"Darlings, I don't believe it!" she had shrieked when Jill, Chris and Prue turned up on her doorstep at ten o'clock with the good news. "This is quite wonderful! Come in. David and I are already having a little celebration between ourselves — we got engaged today — but your news is simply divine!"

Jill was glad that David was out of earshot. Sally appeared to be far more thrilled at the possible return of her stolen property than in the acquisition of a fiancé!

When the five of them were settled with

their drinks Jill was conscious of Prue and Chris radiating misplaced sympathy for herself, and David looking ill at ease. Congratulating him on his newly acquired status had not been easy for Jill; the swift glance which passed between them spoke volumes.

Even now, an hour later, they were avoiding each others eyes; David not wanting the reproachful sympathy he read in Jill's; she hating the ironic self mockery in his.

"But what made you decide to go to the antique shop?" Sally was asking Prue again.

"I just hated the idea of the thieves getting away with it. I figured that though the police's hands were tied by all sorts of technicalities, mine weren't."

"It's a good job I didn't know what you were up to," Jill broke in. "I'd have locked you in your room and thrown away the key."

Prue grinned cheekily. "Why do you think I was so secretive about it? I took the train to Compton Bassett on my afternoon off. I wasn't sure what I was going to do — I just hoped that, by passing myself off as an innocent customer, I could find something out. Gosh, I was so relieved that I didn't come face to face with Dennis Murdoch. He wouldn't have known who I was but I'd have died of fright anyway."

"So you met this Tony person in the shop instead?" Chris asked.

"No, there was just a nice old lady serving there. I'm sure she could have nothing to do with the gang. I'd memorised a few items on the stolen property list and, after poking around a bit as though I was a genuine customer, I asked if she had any more snuff boxes than the ones on display, as my Dad collects them and I wanted to buy a special one for his birthday."

"How clever!" Sally exclaimed. She had heard all of this several times already, but as long as Prue was willing to go on repeating it, Sally was happy to listen.

"Of course, she couldn't help," Prue went on, "but when I'd left the shop, feeling rather a fool for thinking I'd be able to succeed where the police hadn't, this chap followed me into a cafe where I'd gone for a coffee."

"That was where Tony came into the picture. And he offered to get you what you were looking for," Jill said, dying to go home and trying to hurry the narrative along. "I suppose he wanted to make a few bob on the side."

"I don't think it was entirely for the money," Prue said, trying to look modest. "Anyway, he said he'd overheard me in the shop and that he had this friend who'd recently acquired some snuff boxes and he — Tony, that is — might be able to get hold of a couple of them for me to look at."

"I'd love to see Murdoch's face when he discovers that one of his accomplices gave the game away simply in order to impress a pretty face," David mused.

"He won't be pleased," Jill agreed with satisfaction. "What I don't understand, Prue, is why it took you two dates with Tony — Sunday and Monday — to get hold of the snuff box."

Prue blushed. "I didn't enjoy his company, if that's what you're implying — he was horrible. I think he realised that when he'd got me what I was looking for, I wouldn't go out with him again, so he kept putting it off."

"And he only charged you a tenner for a beautiful piece of Fabergé," Jill said wonderingly. "That has to be an all time bargain. He must really have been smitten with you. Well — " she struggled to her feet — "it's all been very exciting but if I don't soon get some sleep I shall drop in my tracks. Come along, Miss Marple, I think you should try and get a good night's rest after all your crime-busting."

They were very quiet on the way home. Jill was too tired to make conversation, Prue was dumbfounded by the news that she would be entitled to the reward if Sally's property was returned, and Chris seemed lost in thought. The news of the engagement appeared to have affected him as deeply as anyone, and Jill wondered with grim amusement where his sympathies lay — with herself because she wasn't marrying David, or with Sally because she was!

The following morning Jill rang Poppy in London to bring her up to date on the latest happenings. After Prue's adventures had been recounted, Jill broke the news of Sally and David's engagement.

"Good grief!" Poppy exclaimed in amazement. "So she's overcome her principles and is marrying for love rather than money."

"Poppy!" Jill protested, laughing at her friend's cynicism. "That's not fair. She was very fond of Charley."

"Possibly," Poppy conceded, "but I'm surprised at David — I thought he was rather keen on you."

Poppy was still the only person in whom Jill confided totally, but yesterday's scene with David was too painful even for her sympathetic ears and Jill merely said, "That's vanity for you. I must have overestimated my charms. By the way, I'll be up in town on Friday. Chris is taking Prue and me to the ballet. She and I are going to spend the whole day there, so perhaps we can get together for lunch?"

"Oh super," Poppy enthused. "You must come straight to our house. I'm looking forward to meeting Prue after all I've heard about her. Speaking of Chris, I suppose there's no way you can maroon him in Foxbridge for a few weeks?"

Jill laughed. "He went back this morning. Why?"

"Miranda, his ex-fiancée, is back in town. Evidently a year of married bliss in Shropshire proved to be eleven months too long for her. I met her prowling around Harrods — and I do mean prowling. I gather from what she said that she'd love to get her claws into Chris again. Poor old love, he doesn't deserve to go through all that grief for a second time."

When Jill finally rang off she noticed that her hands were shaking. Poppy's carefree words kept dancing through her head: "Miranda is back in town; she'd love to get her claws into Chris again."

Jill hadn't been upset by Chris's interest in Sally because she had known, deep down, that it was only superficial, and his behaviour last night had proved that. He was more concerned about whether Sally was doing the right thing rather than how it would affect him personally. He certainly wasn't — how had Poppy put it when she described his reaction to Miranda jilting him? — shattered, devastated.

But that was exactly how Jill felt at the news that, as far as Chris was concerned, London was a jungle stalked by a man-eating redhead. Even now Miranda was probably painting her talons and grooming her mane, ready to swoop on her unsuspecting prey.

Jill sat down, deeply shaken and scared by the sudden blinding knowledge that she loved Chris. She was shaken because she had begun to wonder if she was capable of such intense emotion, and scared because she was certain that she stood as much chance of getting him as she had of flying to the moon.

9

IN the face of the knowledge that she was hopelessly — in the truest sense of the word — in love with Chris Langton, every other occurrence in Jill's life paled by comparison. David Melbury's odd, contrary behaviour lost its power to discomfit her, and though she rejoiced when Prue's amateur sleuthing bore fruit and arrests were made, she found it difficult.

She had, five minutes after meeting Chris and being dazzled by his charm and good looks, decided that she was in no danger of falling for him. And she hadn't been — not immediately. How was she to know that Chris's brilliant and flippant surface was merely the defensive camouflage of a warm, sensitive man who had been badly hurt and was determined not to let it happen again? But as she had got to know him, the brittle layers peeled away and she had been captivated by the real person revealed. And it had happened so slowly she had been unaware of it until a few careless words of gossip on the telephone struck at her heart like an icy dagger.

Over the next couple of days Jill ran endless action replays of her meetings and conversations with Chris over in her mind, searching for clues as to the true nature of their relationship, seeking words or gestures which might indicate that he reciprocated her feelings. But she couldn't find enough crumbs of comfort to keep a sparrow alive.

Luckily Prue was too wrapped up in her role as resident heroine, and with planning ways in which to spend her reward money, to notice that Jill was quiet and preoccupied, but Sally did.

"You look glum," she observed, when she and Jill encountered each other in the town on Thursday morning. "Been crossed in love?"

It was a flippant question but Jill misunderstood and stared at her in consternation. Was it that obvious?

"Just joking, sweetie," Sally apologised. "Though your face tells me I've hit a raw nerve. Having problems with that lovely

327

Chris, are you? You know, I shall always wonder if I did the right thing in deciding to settle for David, but I suppose it's all for the best."

Jill was shaken out of her preoccupation. Her expression must have betrayed shock and Sally gave a rueful smile. She indicated that they should sit on one of the benches lining the main shopping thoroughfare and continued, "Don't look so appalled, Jill, I didn't mean it to sound that bad. David and I are very fond of each other in our own way. And we'll make a go of it, not despite our faults, but probably because of them. We're very much alike, David and I; we're selfish, a little lonely and we've both got something missing from our emotional make-up. I don't know how to define it; tenderness, warmth. Whatever it was with me, it died with Charley."

She turned to Jill, her pretty face more pensive and earnest than Jill had ever seen. "I really did love Charley. I know what everybody thinks, that I married him for his money, but it isn't true. I'd have married him even if he hadn't had a bean. I don't know if I'll ever quite get over losing him."

Jill was silent. She had never been one of Sally's detractors in that respect and had no reason to feel guilty but she was shaken by the hidden depth of Sally's feelings.

"As for David," Sally went on, "I suspect that part of him — the loving part — died in the accident. Still — " she rose and smiled wryly down at Jill — "I suppose I stand as good a chance as anybody of making him happy — and vice versa, of course."

'Not just anybody,' thought Jill miserably as she watched Sally walk briskly away. 'He offered me the chance and I turned it down. How awful that my relationships are so one sided; not feeling enough for David and feeling too much for Chris. Do other people have the same trouble? I'm sure they don't or the human race would be extinct by now.'

★ ★ ★

Leaving Pooch once again with the obliging Melanie, Jill and Prue caught

329

an early train into London the following morning and made their way to Poppy and Miles Hatherford's house in Hampstead. There was a good deal of mutual curiosity between the two women who had heard so much about each other but hadn't met, and Jill was delighted — and relieved — when her cousin and best friend took an instant liking to each other.

"Isn't she great?" Prue said when she and Jill had a few minutes alone. "I can quite understand how you had such fun together when she shared the flat with you."

And later, when Prue was out of earshot, Poppy exclaimed, "You didn't tell me how sweet and pretty she is. I was expecting a King's Road freak but she reminds me of you when we were that age. Gosh, that makes me feel old."

In order not to have to rush to catch the last train, they were to spend the night at Poppy's. After a leisurely day, shopping, lunching and having their hair done, they repaired to the spare room to dress.

Jill had bought a pale yellow silk dress, very plain with shoe-string straps, which showed off her tan and the subtle ash and gold tones of her fashionably dressed hair. Her agate dress ring and some simple gold chains completed the picture.

"You look marvellous," Prue said, returning from the bathroom as Jill was finishing her make-up, "all gold and shimmery like — "

"A Christmas tree?" Jill asked, not entirely joking. She'd got out of the habit of dressing up to quite such a degree. She had to admit that the effect was pleasing but couldn't help wishing that she had red hair and was called Miranda!

"Aren't you going to get ready?" she asked Prue, who was sitting on the bed in her robe, staring into space. "Chris will be here to collect us in half an hour."

Prue screwed up her face and pressed a hand to her abdomen. "I don't think I should go. I've just been sick. It must have been that prawn cocktail I had at lunch."

"Oh no, poor you!" Jill went and sat beside her cousin. "Should we call a doctor? I'll stay here with you."

"No, no!" Prue objected violently.

"You mustn't do that. Somebody's got to go with Chris and I'll be fine here with Poppy."

"But it's your treat, love. He bought the tickets so that you should see Firebird. Are you sure you're ill?" Jill looked closely at Prue's peachy complexion. "You aren't at all pale."

"I'm flushed from the shower," Prue mumbled. "I — er — don't feel too bad but I don't want to risk being taken ill in the middle of the performance. You go ahead without me."

Prue was adamant and Jill puzzled, even more so when she departed with Chris, half an hour later, leaving Prue energetically romping on the living room floor with baby Laura.

In the light of her recent knowledge, Jill was not looking forward to the evening, and the absence of a third party made it worse. Her attitude towards Chris had always been supremely relaxed; now it was the complete opposite. He was, presumably because it was a formal occasion, an attentive escort and this contributed to Jill's discomfort.

He had, on arrival, presented her

with a tiny box of exquisite, handmade chocolates and a single, perfect golden rose. His complimentary comparison of herself to the rose died a sad death and their embarrassment was furthered by her not having anywhere suitable to fasten it. She eventually managed to fix it on her gold embroidered evening bag.

The conversation also left a great deal to be desired. They had never discussed anything seriously and it was unthinkable that they should do so now, but their usual joking and teasing had, to Jill's ears, a false ring to it. During the taxi ride they became less and less communicative and arrived at the theatre in a state of mutual unease.

"Are you very worried about Prue?" Chris asked as they took their seats.

"Not at all," Jill replied truthfully and then wished that she had seized on the white lie to explain her mood.

"Are you feeling well yourself?" he persisted.

She nodded. "I'm fine, thanks." To have pleaded indisposition as an excuse for her solemnity would have meant encouraging even more of those frowning sideways glances he was giving her.

Firebird, dazzling to the eye and ravishing to the ear, was a consolation and distraction. Too much of a distraction, Jill decided when she was required to applaud and found she had been clutching Chris's hand. She dropped it quickly enough to earn herself another puzzled glance.

In another taxi, this one bearing them to the restaurant where he had booked a table for supper, Chris said, "I wish you'd talk to me about whatever it is that's troubling you, angel. It's not as if I can't guess what's wrong."

'Want to bet,' Jill thought unhappily and then felt a thrill of horror as he went on, "I know all about unrequited love; I could write a book about it and I'd end up by saying that you do get over it, honestly."

Jill stared blindly out of the window at the brightly lit shop windows flashing past, and felt her palms go damp with embarrassment. How did he know? What had she said to give herself away?

"I told you David Melbury would cause you nothing but grief but you wouldn't listen. Still, why should you take advice? I never would."

Jill opened her mouth to correct him but the taxi drew to a halt and Chris was distracted by the business of paying the driver. The large, self-consciously fashionable restaurant had been chosen by Prue because it was reputed to be patronised by the glitterati. There was indeed an impressive sprinkling of the so-called beautiful people among the chrome and glass and tropical foliage, but Jill had eyes only for the beautiful person she was with.

"But, Chris, you don't understand!" she muttered urgently as they were shown to their table. "You're completely wrong about David . . . "

The casually dressed young waiter gave her a sympathetic smile and she fell into a discreet silence until he had presented the menus and departed.

"About David," she began again. "I've never been remotely in love with him . . ."

Chris's eyes widened. "But — I thought . . . "

This time the interruption came from the neon-lit bar. A tall, glossy redhead, dressed in a skimpily-cut black dress, detached herself from a noisy group and swooped on their table with a cry of "Chris darling! I've been hoping to see you! I've missed you so dreadfully!"

Chris rose and greeted her with equal enthusiasm. "Miranda! You look wonderful!"

Jill tried not to watch as Miranda twined herself about him like some glamorous form of poison ivy. What a horrible coincidence. Oh well, it would save her feeling obliged to explain about David. Chris wasn't really interested; he was just being polite; the whole evening had been an exercise in politeness. Roses and chocolates, indeed!

Jill detached the wilting flower from her bag and stuck it in her glass of mineral water to revive it. Poor thing, it looked exactly how she felt; out of place and utterly miserable. It had been clever of Chris to match it so well to her outfit. What had he bought to go with Prue's red dress?

Jill frowned as she tried to remember. He hadn't brought anything for Prue! He'd arrived on the doorstep, supposedly expecting to escort two women, bearing only one rose. And, it had just occurred to her, there hadn't been an empty seat beside them at the ballet. To have disposed of it he would have had to inform the box office well before the performance. He'd known that Prue wasn't coming!

Puzzled, Jill looked up to where Chris and Miranda were still talking, locked in a passionate embrace. Or, rather, Miranda was embracing and talking, hanging on to him, yakking nineteen to the dozen; Chris was standing with his arms at his sides, a glazed look on his face. When he met Jill's gaze he rolled his eyes in a comical grimace of helplessness and boredom.

It was the first natural, spontaneous gesture he had made all evening and Jill began to laugh, almost hysterically, with relief. His behaviour was not that of a man confronting the object of his unrequited passion. And when he laughed with her, his brown eyes warm and amused, as though they shared a secret, Jill felt a tiny seed of joy begin to blossom inside her.

He unwound Miranda's arms from his

neck and, with a few words and a gentle push, sent her back to her friends at the bar. As her elegant back retreated, Jill's hopes advanced.

"My ex-fiancee," Chris announced blandly, rejoining Jill. "I get the impression she's rather keen on a reconciliation."

Thick lashes hid his eyes but Jill had the feeling that he was watching her intently, gauging her reaction.

"What did you tell her?" she asked, studying the menu and feigning disinterest in his affairs.

"I said: no thank you, we were never suited and I'm in love with somebody else; properly in love this time, not just infatuated."

She watched her hands playing with tassel on the menu. "Does this other woman know how you feel about her?"

"I don't think so. And I don't know if I dare tell her. She's an obstinate, independent creature who refuses to take me seriously. I thought it was because she loved somebody else but it turns out I was wrong. So — " he heaved a theatrical sigh — "I suppose I'm just not her type. What do you think?"

Jill deliberately let her gaze wander around the restaurant. Miranda was back with her friends, not one whit put out by her disappointment. "Perhaps this obstinate woman — whoever she is — has recently realised how mixed up she was. Perhaps she was so busy not falling in love with one man that she didn't notice she'd fallen for you." Her voice trembled with a mixture of tears and laughter.

"Had she — I mean, you?" Chris dropped the joking pretence and took her hand. "Jill darling, I've been so miserable, imagining that you were breaking your heart over David. I thought tonight would be an opportunity to make a fuss of you and perhaps make you forget the trauma of his choosing Sally. I wanted to make you feel special."

Jill looked around the artificial setting and thought back over the unnatural formality of the evening. "It almost didn't work. I'm sure there are much nicer ways of making me feel special."

Chris also glanced around. "It's horrible, isn't it? But blame your cousin — it was her choice. Shall we skip supper? There's a nice secluded square just around the corner."

The little square was one of the charming, grassy oases which occur unexpectedly in the middle of London's noise and glitter. A border of nicotiana scented the night air and the harsh street lighting fell softly through a veil of beech leaves. As Chris and Jill seated themselves on a wooden bench, a few leaves drifted down, a reminder that autumn wasn't far away.

Jill felt strangely shy as she asked him, "Why have you waited until now before saying . . . ? Telling me . . . "

"That I love you? Because I was convinced that you were in love with David. Were you, darling?"

She shook her head, smiling. "No — at least, not since I was sixteen. But he rather fascinated me still, I must admit. It's all over now, though; I've got him completely out of my system. What about you and Miranda? I nearly died when I heard she was back in town."

Chris grinned. "Poppy told you, did she? She promised she would. I was hoping that even if it didn't send you into a froth of jealousy, you might at least feel sorry for me. I couldn't believe my luck when she came prancing over tonight."

"You conniving rat! I wouldn't be surprised to hear you set the whole thing up. Incidentally — " she snatched her hand away from his and frowned at him with mock severity — "exactly how did you bribe Prue to pull that food poisoning stunt?"

Chris looked harassed. "Crikey, she drives a hard bargain. I'm to give her driving lessons and then talk you into not going potty when she buys herself a sports car with Sally's reward money."

"I'll worry about it when it happens," she said indulgently. "It's impossible to feel happy and angry at the same time. Would you like to have another try at making me feel special?"

"First tell me you love me," he demanded.

Jill told him, with words and then actions which left neither of them in any doubt as to how they both felt.

"Are you sure you haven't been brooding over David this evening?"

341

Chris asked again.

Jill was surprised and a little touched by his need for reassurance. It was the last thing she would have expected from the elegant, blase young man she had met at the country club. The sophisticated stranger, who had complained about his obligation to meet a 'boring old spinster', was gone. She suspected that he had existed only as a facade behind which Chris could hide. One day, when he no longer felt the need to ask, she would tell Chris about her muddled feelings for David but that was in the future.

"David who?" she gently teased. "There's been only one man making me feel broody lately, and that's you. When Poppy rang and told me you were in danger of being gobbled up by Miranda, I nearly died." Jill shuddered at the memory and snuggled closer to him. "How Poppy will crow when she finds out that all her scheming and conniving has worked. She engineered the whole thing, you know, long before you and I set eyes on each other. She should start a dating agency — she'd be a terrific success."

"Possibly," Chris agreed, "but I think

she should rest on her laurels. If she worked at it for the next thousand years, she'd never make a more perfect match."

THE END

THE WILDERNESS WALK
Sheila Bishop

Stifling unpleasant memories of a misbegotten romance in Cleave with Lord Francis Aubrey, Lavinia goes on holiday there with her sister. The two women are thrust into a romantic intrigue involving none other than Lord Francis.

THE RELUCTANT GUEST
Rosalind Brett

Ann Calvert went to spend a month on a South African farm with Theo Borland and his sister. They both proved to be different from her first idea of them, and there was Storr Peterson — the most disturbing man she had ever met.

ONE ENCHANTED SUMMER
Anne Tedlock Brooks

A tale of mystery and romance and a girl who found both during one enchanted summer.

CLOUD OVER MALVERTON
Nancy Buckingham

Dulcie soon realises that something is seriously wrong at Malverton, and when violence strikes she is horrified to find herself under suspicion of murder.

AFTER THOUGHTS
Max Bygraves

The Cockney entertainer tells stories of his East End childhood, of his RAF days, and his post-war showbusiness successes and friendships with fellow comedians.

MOONLIGHT
AND MARCH ROSES
D. Y. Cameron

Lynn's search to trace a missing girl takes her to Spain, where she meets Clive Hendon. While untangling the situation, she untangles her emotions and decides on her own future.